spy school

STUART GIBBS

spy school

Simon & Schuster Books for Young Readers

New York London Toronto Sydney New Delhi

SIMON & SCHUSTER BOOKS FOR YOUNG READERS
An imprint of Simon & Schuster Children's Publishing Division
1230 Avenue of the Americas, New York, New York 10020
This book is a work of fiction. Any references to historical events, real people, or real places are used fictitiously. Other names, characters, places, and events are products of the author's imagination, and any resemblance to actual events or places or persons, living or dead, is entirely coincidental.
Copyright © 2012 by Stuart Gibbs
All rights reserved, including the right of reproduction in whole or in part in any form.
SIMON & SCHUSTER BOOKS FOR YOUNG READERS is a trademark of Simon & Schuster, Inc.
For information about special discounts for bulk purchases, please contact Simon & Schuster Special Sales at 1-866-506-1949 or business@simonandschuster.com.
The Simon & Schuster Speakers Bureau can bring authors to your live event. For more information or to book an event, contact the Simon & Schuster Speakers Bureau at 1-866-248-3049 or visit our website at www.simonspeakers.com.
Also available in a Simon & Schuster Books for Young Readers hardcover edition
Book design by Lucy Ruth Cummins
The text for this book is set in Adobe Garamond.
Manufactured in the United States of America
0319 OFF
First Simon & Schuster Books for Young Readers paperback edition April 2013
20
The Library of Congress has cataloged the hardcover edition as follows:
Gibbs, Stuart, 1969–
Spy school / Stuart Gibbs. — 1st ed.
p. cm.
Summary: Twelve-year-old Ben Ripley leaves his public middle school to attend the CIA's highly secretive Espionage Academy, which everyone is told is an elite science school.
ISBN 978-1-4424-2182-0 (hardcover)
[1. Spies—Fiction. 2. Schools—Fiction.] I. Title.
PZ7.G339236Sp 2012
[Fic]—dc23
2011015023
ISBN 978-1-4424-2183-7 (pbk)
ISBN 978-1-4424-2184-4 (eBook)

To my wonderful wife, Suzanne

acknowledgments

This is a story I've wanted to tell for a long, long time. I first thought up the idea of a spy school on the playground in elementary school, and while the actual story has changed a great deal since then, my desire to share it hasn't. Therefore I am greatly indebted to my wonderful agent, Jennifer Joel, and my equally wonderful editor, Courtney Bongiolatti, for making this happen. Thank you both. Thank you, thank you, thank you.

contents

From:
Office of CIA Internal Investigations
CIA Headquarters
Langley, Virginia

To:
████████████████
Director of Covert Affairs
The White House
Washington, DC

Classified Documents Enclosed
Security Level AA2
For Your Eyes Only

As part of the continuing investigation into Operation Creeping Badger,
the following pages have been transcribed from 53 hours of debriefings
of Mr. Benjamin Ripley, aka Smokescreen, age 12, a first year student at
the Academy of Espionage.

Mr. Ripley's acceptance to the academy, while unprecedented, was
sanctioned by ████████████████████████ and ███████████████,
Director of the CIA, as part of the operation.

As Operation Creeping Badger did not proceed as planned, given the
events of ███
████████████████, this investigation has been launched to determine
exactly what went wrong, why it went wrong, and who should be
terminated for it.

After reading these documents, they are to be destroyed immediately,
in accordance with CIA Security Directive 163-12A. No discussion of
these pages will be tolerated, except during the review, which will be
conducted in ██
█████████████████. Please note that no weapons will be allowed at said
meeting.

I look forward to hearing your thoughts.

████████████████
Director of Internal Investigations

Cc:
████████████████
██████████████████████
████████████████
██████████████████████

RECRUITMENT

Ripley Residence
2107 Mockingbird Road
Vienna, Virginia
January 16
1530 hours

"Hello, Ben," said the man in my living room. **"My** name is Alexander Hale. I work for the CIA."

And just like that, my life became interesting.

It hadn't been, up till then. Not by a long shot. That day had been a prime example: day 4,583, seven months into the twelfth year of my mundane existence. I had dragged myself out of bed, eaten breakfast, gone to middle school, been bored in class, stared at girls I was too embarrassed to approach, had lunch, slogged through gym, fallen asleep in math, been harassed by Dirk the Jerk, taken the bus home . . .

And found a man in a tuxedo sitting on the couch.

I didn't doubt he was a spy for a second. Alexander Hale looked exactly like I'd always imagined a spy would. A tiny bit older, perhaps—he seemed about fifty—but still suave and debonair. He had a small scar on his chin—from a bullet, I guessed, or maybe something more exotic, like a crossbow. There was something very James Bond about him; I could imagine he'd been in a car chase on the way over and taken out the bad guys without breaking a sweat.

My parents weren't home. They never were when I got back from school. Alexander had obviously "let himself in." The photo album from our family vacation to Virginia Beach sat open on the coffee table before him.

"Am I in trouble?" I asked.

Alexander laughed. "For what? You've never done anything wrong in your life. Unless you count the time you spiked Dirk Dennett's Pepsi with Ex-Lax—and frankly, that kid was asking for it."

My eyes widened in surprise. "How did you know that?"

"I'm a spy. It's my job to know things. Do you have anything to drink?"

"Uh, sure." My mind quickly cataloged every beverage

in the house. Although I had no idea what this man was doing there, I found myself desperately wanting to impress him. "My folks have all kinds of stuff. What would you like? A martini?"

Alexander laughed again. "This isn't the movies, kid. I'm on the clock."

I blushed, feeling foolish. "Oh. Right. Water?"

"I was thinking more like an energy drink. Something with electrolytes, just in case I need to leap into action. I had to ditch some undesirables on my way over here."

"Undesirables?" I tried to sound cool, as though I discussed things like this every day. "What sort of . . . ?"

"I'm afraid that information is classified."

"Of course. That makes sense. Gatorade?"

"That'd be grand."

I headed to the kitchen.

Alexander followed. "The Agency has had its eye on you for some time," he said.

I paused, surprised, the refrigerator door half open. "Why?"

"For starters, you asked us to."

"I did? When?"

"How many times have you accessed our website?"

I grimaced, feeling foolish once again. "Seven hundred twenty-eight."

Alexander looked the tiniest bit intrigued. "That's exactly right. Usually you merely play the games on the kids' page—at which you performed very well, by the way—but you've also browsed the employment and internship pages with some regularity. Ergo, you've considered a career as a spy. And when you express an interest in the CIA, the CIA becomes interested in *you*." Alexander pulled a thick envelope from inside his tuxedo and set it on the kitchen counter. "We've been impressed."

The envelope was marked, *To be hand-delivered ONLY to Mr. Benjamin Ripley*. There were three security seals on it, one of which required a steak knife to open. Inside was a thick wad of paper. The first page had only one sentence: *Destroy these documents immediately after reading.*

The second page began: *Dear Mr. Ripley: It is my great privilege to accept you to the Academy of Espionage of the Central Intelligence Agency, effective immediately. . . .*

I set the letter down, at once stunned, thrilled, and confused. My whole life, I'd dreamt of being a spy. And yet . . .

"You think it's a joke," Alexander said, reading my mind.

"Well . . . yes. I've never heard of the CIA's Academy of Espionage."

"That's because it's top secret. But I assure you it exists. I graduated from there myself. A fine institution, dedicated to creating the agents of tomorrow today. Congratulations!" Alexander raised his glass of Gatorade and flashed a blinding smile.

I clinked glasses with him. He waited for me to drink some of mine before downing his, which I figured was a habit you picked up after a lifetime of having people try to poison you.

I caught a glimpse of my own reflection in the microwave behind Alexander—and doubt descended on me. It didn't seem possible that he and I could have been selected by the same organization. Alexander was handsome, athletic, sophisticated, and cool. I wasn't. How could I be qualified to keep the world safe for democracy when I'd been shaken down for my lunch money three times that week alone?

"But how——?" I began.

". . . did you get into the academy when you didn't even apply?"

"Er—yes."

"Applications merely provide opportunities for you to tell the institution you're applying to about yourself. The CIA already has all the information it needs." Alexander removed a small handheld computer from his pocket and consulted it. "For example, you're a straight-A student who speaks three languages and has Level 16 math skills."

"What's that mean?"

"What is 98,261 times 147?"

"14,444,367." I didn't even have to think about it. I have

a gift for mathematics—and, as a result, an uncanny ability to always know exactly what time it is—although for much of my life, I hadn't realized this was anything special. I thought *everyone* could do complex mathematical equations in their heads . . . or instantly calculate how many days, weeks, or minutes they'd been alive. I was 3,832 days old when I found out otherwise.

"*That's* Level 16," Alexander said, then looked at his computer again. "According to our files, you also aced your STIQ exams, have a strong aptitude for electronics, and harbor a severe crush on a Miss Elizabeth Pasternak—although, sadly, she appears to have no idea you exist."

I'd assumed as much about Elizabeth, but it still hurt to hear it confirmed. By the CIA, no less. So I tried to divert attention. "Stick exams? I don't remember taking those."

"You wouldn't. You didn't even know you *were* taking them. Standardized Test Inserted Questions: STIQ. The CIA places them in every standardized test to assess potential espionage aptitude. You've gotten every one right since third grade."

"You insert your own questions in the standardized tests? Does the Department of Education know that?"

"I doubt it. They don't know much of anything over at Education." Alexander set his empty glass in the sink and rubbed his hands together excitedly. "Well, enough chitchat.

Let's get you packed, shall we? You have a busy afternoon ahead."

"You mean, we're going *now*?"

Alexander turned back to me, already halfway to the stairs. "You scored in the ninety-nine point ninth percentile on the perception section of your STIQs. What part of 'effective immediately' did you not understand?"

I stammered a bit; there were still a hundred questions tumbling around in my brain, vying to be asked at once. "I . . . uh . . . well. . . Why am I packing? How far away is this academy?"

"Oh, not far at all. Just across the Potomac in DC. But becoming a spy is a full-time job, so all students are required to live on campus. Your training lasts six years, starting in the equivalent of seventh grade and going through twelfth. You'll be a first year, obviously." With that, Alexander bounded up the steps to my room.

When I got there twenty seconds later, he already had my suitcase open and was casting a disdainful eye on the contents of my closet. "Not a single decent suit." He sighed. He selected a few sweaters and tossed them on my bed.

"Is the academy on a different schedule than normal schools?" I asked.

"No."

"Then why are they accepting me *now*? It's the middle of

the school year." I pointed to the four inches of fresh snow piled on my windowsill.

For the first time since I'd met him, Alexander Hale appeared at a loss for words. It didn't last long. Less than a second. As though there were something he wanted to say but didn't.

Instead, he told me, "There was a sudden opening."

"Someone quit?"

"Flunked out. Your name was next on the list. Do you have any weapons?"

In retrospect, I realize the question was designed to distract me from the current topic. It served its purpose extremely well. "Uh . . . I have a slingshot."

"Slingshots are for squirrels. We don't fight many squirrels in the CIA. I meant *real* weapons. Guns, knives, perhaps a pair of nunchucks . . ."

"No."

Alexander shook his head slightly, as though disappointed. "Well, it's no matter. The school armory can loan you some. In the meantime, I suppose *this* will suffice." He pulled my dusty old tennis racket from the back of the closet and swung it like a sword. "Just in case there's trouble, you know."

For the first time it occurred to me that Alexander might be armed himself. There was a slight bulge in his tuxedo, right below his left armpit, which I now took to be a gun.

In that moment, the entire encounter with him—which had merely been strange and exciting so far—became slightly unsettling as well.

"Maybe before I make any big decisions, I should discuss all this with my parents," I said.

Alexander wheeled on me. "Out of the question. The existence of the academy is classified. No one is to know you are attending. Not your parents, not your best friends, not Elizabeth Pasternak. *No one.* As far as they're concerned, you'll be attending St. Smithen's Science Academy for Boys and Girls."

"A science academy?" I frowned. "I'll be training to save the world, but everyone's gonna think I'm a dork."

"Isn't that pretty much how everyone thinks of you now?"

I winced. He *did* know a lot about me. "They'll think I'm an even bigger dork."

Alexander sat on my bed and looked me in the eye. "Being an elite operative demands sacrifice," he said. "This is only the beginning. Your training won't be easy. And if you succeed, your *life* won't be easy. A lot of people can't hack it. So if you want to back out . . . this is your chance."

I assumed this was a final test. The last step in my recruitment. A chance to prove I wouldn't be dissuaded by the threat of hard work and tough times ahead.

It wasn't. Alexander was being honest with me, but I was too caught up in the excitement of being chosen to notice. I wanted to be just like Alexander Hale. I wanted to be suave and debonair. I wanted to "let myself in" to people's homes with a gun casually tucked inside my tuxedo. I wanted to ditch undesirables, keep the world safe, and impress the heck out of Elizabeth Pasternak. I wouldn't have even minded a rakish crossbow scar on my chin.

And so, I stared back into his steel gray eyes and made the worst decision of my life.

"I'm in," I said.

INITIATION

CIA Academy of Espionage

Washington, DC

January 16

1700 hours

The academy didn't look a thing like what I expected an institution that taught espionage to look like. Which, of course, was the whole point. Instead, it looked like a dowdy old prep school that might have been popular around World War II but had long since lost its mojo. It was located in a similarly dowdy, rarely visited corner of Washington, DC, hidden from the world by a high stone wall. The only thing that seemed the least bit suspicious about it was the cluster of security guards at the front gate, but since our nation's capital is also its murder capital, extra security around a private school wouldn't raise many eyebrows.

Inside, the grounds were surprisingly large. There were vast expanses of lawn that I assumed would be beautiful in spring, although they were currently buried under a foot of snow. And beyond the buildings stood a large, pristine swath of forest, untouched since the days when our forefathers had decided a fetid, malaria-ridden swamp on the Potomac River was the perfect place to build our nation's capital.

The buildings themselves were ugly and gothic, trying to imitate the majesty of places like Oxford and Harvard but failing miserably. Though braced by flying buttresses and dotted with gargoyles, they were still gray and uninteresting, designed so that anyone who accidentally stumbled upon St. Smithen's Science Academy would turn his back and never think of it again.

But compared to the squat cement slab where I went to middle school, the campus was gorgeous. I arrived with Alexander at an inauspicious time, minutes before nightfall in the dead of winter. The light was bleak, the sky was leaden, and the buildings were shrouded in shadow. And yet, I was thrilled. The fact that we'd come in Alexander's customized luxury sedan with a few extra buttons on the dashboard probably heightened my excitement. (Though he'd warned me to keep my hands off them for fear of launching heavy artillery into rush-hour traffic.)

My parents hadn't protested my leaving much. Alexander had wowed them with his pitch for the "science" academy and reassured them that I was going to be only a few miles away. Mom and Dad were both proud of me for getting into such a prestigious institution—and thrilled that they wouldn't have to pay for it. (Alexander told them I'd earned a full scholarship, and he told *me* the whole tab was picked up by the U.S. government.) Still, they'd been surprised that I had to leave so quickly—and disappointed that Mom couldn't even make me a farewell dinner. Mom was big on commemorative dinners, throwing them for things as mundane as my getting elected captain of the school chess team, even though I was the only student on the school chess team. But Alexander had quelled their anxiety by promising I could return home to visit soon. (When they'd asked if they could visit me on the campus, he'd assured them they could, although he'd artfully avoided telling them exactly *when*.)

Mike Brezinski hadn't been quite so enthusiastic about my going. Mike has been my best friend since first grade, though if we'd met later in life, we probably wouldn't have been friends at all. Mike had grown into one of those cool underachievers who should have been in all advanced classes but preferred remedial ones because he didn't have to work in them. Middle school was one big joke to him. "You're going to a science academy?" he'd asked when I called him with the news, making no attempt to hide his disgust. "Why don't you just get 'loser' tattooed on your forehead?"

It took every ounce of restraint I had not to tell him the truth. More than anyone, Mike would have been blown away by the idea that *I* had been selected for training by the CIA. As kids, we'd spent untold hours reenacting James Bond movies on the playground. But I couldn't reveal a thing; Alexander was sitting in my room, casually eavesdropping on my phone call. Instead, I'd only been able to say, "It's not as lame as you think."

"No," Mike had replied. "It's probably lamer."

So as I arrived at the Academy of Espionage, escorted by an honest-to-God federal agent, I couldn't help but think that, if Mike were there, for the first time in our lives he'd be jealous of *me*. The campus seemed full of promise, intrigue, and excitement.

"Wow," I said, my nose pressed against the car window.

"This is nothing," Alexander told me. "There's far more here than meets the eye."

"What do you mean?"

Alexander didn't answer. When I turned back to him, his normally confident expression had clouded.

"What's wrong?" I asked.

"I don't see any students."

"They're not all at dinner?"

"Dinner's not for another hour. This period is reserved for sports, physical conditioning, and self-defense training. Campus ought to be crawling with people right now." Alexander suddenly braked in front of a rambling four-story building with a sign denoting it as the Armistead Dormitory. "When I say so, run for that doorway. I'll cover you." It turned out, there *was* a gun holstered under his left armpit. He snapped it out and reached for my door handle.

"Wait!" Within a second, I'd gone from blissful to terrified. "Isn't it safer to stay in the car?"

"Who's the agent here? You or me?"

"You."

"Then run!" In one fluid motion Alexander popped my door open and practically shoved me out it.

I hit the ground running. The stone path to the dormitory was slick with slush trampled by a hundred pairs of shoes. My feet slipped and skidded in it.

Something cracked in the distance. A tiny explosion erupted in the snow to my left.

Someone was shooting at me!

I immediately began to question my decision to attend the academy.

Another series of cracks echoed in the cold air, this time

from behind me. Alexander was shooting back. Or, at least, I *assumed* he was. I didn't dare turn around to see for fear that it'd waste precious milliseconds that could be better spent running for my life.

A bullet ricocheted off the ground by my feet.

I hit the dormitory door at full speed. It flew open, and I tumbled into a small security area. There was a second, more secure door ahead next to a glassed-in security booth, but the door hung ajar and the glass was pocked with three neat, round bullet holes. I scrambled through and found myself in an open lounge area.

It was the type of place students would normally have been hanging out. There were ratty couches, an old television, a lopsided pool table, and some ancient video games. Hallways extended from it on both sides, and a weathered grand staircase led up to—

Something suddenly swept my feet out from under me. I landed flat on my back. A split second later someone dropped on me, sheathed entirely in black except for the eyes. Each knee pinioned one of my arms to the ground. A hand slapped over my mouth before I could scream.

"Who are you?" my attacker hissed.

"B-B-B-Benjamin Ripley," I sputtered. "I'm a student here."

"I've never seen you before."

"I only got accepted this afternoon," I explained, and then thought to add, "Please don't kill me."

My attacker groaned. "A newbie? Now?! This day just keeps getting better." Now that the voice was inflected with sarcasm rather than aggression, it was higher than I'd expected. I looked at the body sitting on my chest and realized it was slim with curves.

"You're a girl," I said.

"Wow," she replied. "No wonder you got accepted. Your powers of deduction are amazing." She pulled her mask back, revealing her face.

I wouldn't have thought my heart could have beat any faster than it had while racing for my life from a hail of gunfire, but it suddenly sped up to a whole new level.

Elizabeth Pasternak was no longer the most beautiful girl I'd ever seen.

The girl sitting on my chest appeared to be a few years older than me, maybe fourteen or fifteen, with thick dark hair and incredibly blue eyes. Her skin was flawless, her cheekbones were sculpted, and her lips were full. She was slight of build—almost delicate—and yet she'd been powerful enough to flatten me in half a second. She even *smelled* incredible, an intoxicating combination of lilacs and gunpowder. But perhaps the most attractive thing about her was how calm and confident she was in the midst of a life-or-death situation. She seemed far more annoyed that I'd stumbled into the action than by the idea that bullets were flying outside.

"Do you have a weapon on you?" she asked.

"No."

"Can you use a gun?"

"I can handle my cousin's BB gun pretty well. . . ."

She sighed heavily, then unzipped her flak jacket, revealing a sleek leather bandolier across her chest bristling with weapons: guns, knives, Chinese throwing stars, grenades. She bypassed all of these and selected a blunt little object for me. "This is a Taser. It's not effective over long range, but on the plus side, you can't accidentally kill me with it." She slapped it into my hand, gave me a quick tutorial—"On/off switch. Trigger. Contact points."—then stood and motioned for me to follow her.

I did. It wasn't as though I had any other ideas. We passed the grand staircase and headed down the south hall of the dormitory. The girl seemed to know what she was doing, so I felt slightly safer being with her. I mimicked her moves, creeping along as she did, holding my Taser the same way she held her gun.

As it was my first action sequence, I wasn't quite sure what the protocol was. It seemed I should introduce myself. "By the way, I'm Benjamin."

"So you said. I'll make you a deal. If we survive this incident, then we can get to know each other."

"Okay. What's going on?"

"Apparently, we've had a security breach. There was an assembly on diplomacy for the entire student body this afternoon. The enemy infiltrated the campus during it and surrounded the assembly hall. All students and faculty are being held hostage inside."

"How'd you escape?"

"I didn't. I'd ditched the assembly. I could give a hoot about diplomacy."

"Is anyone else with you?"

"As far as I know, it's only you and me. I tried calling for backup, but the enemy is jamming all transmissions somehow."

"How many of them are there?"

"I've counted forty-one. So far. Those I've seen are very professional, heavily armed, and extremely dangerous."

I gulped. "I've been here only five minutes, and I'm supposed to face an entire platoon of deadly commandos with only a Taser?"

For the first time since I'd met her, the girl smiled. "Welcome to spy school," she said.

CONFRONTATION

Nathan Hale Administration Building

January 16

1710 hours

Thinking you might be ambushed by enemy operatives at any second is a lousy frame of mind to be in for your first school tour. Although I followed the girl past many locations that would be important to me if I survived, I couldn't focus on any of them. Meanwhile, the girl remained amazingly composed given the circumstances, even pointing out things of interest along the way, as though this were the standard orientation.

"This is the only dormitory for the school," she informed me as we crept through the first-floor hallway, weapons at the ready. "All three hundred students live here. It was built over a century ago, so as you've probably noticed, its enemy defense systems are lousy. Plus, the plumbing is prehistoric.

"The mess hall is over there. Mealtimes are promptly at 0700, 1300, and 1800 hours . . . Now we're heading into the south passage between the dorm and the admin building. It's usually faster to go outside, but this way is better when the weather's bad—or when there are enemy snipers on the property."

There was the distant sound of gunfire outside. Even though it was taking place more than one hundred yards away on the other side of a thick stone wall, I ducked reflexively. This provoked yet another sigh from the girl.

"Wait!" I said. In all the excitement I'd forgotten something. "We're not alone here. I came with Alexander Hale."

I'd expected her to be relieved, maybe even thrilled. But to my surprise, she seemed irritated instead. "Where is he?"

"Outside. Fighting those snipers. I think he saved my life earlier."

"I'm sure he'll think that too," she said.

We reached a fork in the passage where windows opened onto the snow-covered lawns. The girl signaled me to stay low, then peered through the glass. It had grown too dark for me to make out anything other than the silhouettes of buildings, but she seemed to see something. "They have the entire campus perimeter covered," she frowned. "We're not getting off the property. So here's the plan: There's an emergency radio beacon on the top floor of the administration building." She nodded toward a five-story gothic structure that loomed immediately south of us. "It's a direct link to Agency headquarters. So old school, the enemy probably doesn't even know it still exists. If we can make it there, we can probably call for backup."

"Sounds good." I tried my best to sound calm, even though I was growing more terrified by the minute.

"Stay close and do what I tell you." The girl started down the left fork of the hall but paused to point to the right. "The gym's down there, by the way. And the firing range, just for future reference."

I followed her, my head ducked below the windows, fearing imminent attack. My first gunfight wasn't going the way I'd expected at all. Where were all the bad guys? I wondered. Were we cleverly circumventing them, or were they waiting to ambush us? Where was Alexander Hale, and why hadn't the girl been happy to hear about him? And perhaps most important . . .

"Is there a men's room anywhere nearby?" I asked. "I really have to pee." This would be the first time I experienced what is generally referred to in spy school as "Hogarth's theory of fear-based urination": The amount of danger you are in is directly proportional to your need to pee. Abraham Hogarth was one of the CIA's first operatives and, thus, one of the original professors at spy school. He'd written the essential espionage textbook based on his experiences (and he was rumored to always wear an adult diaper, just in case trouble arose).

The girl sighed once again. "Why didn't you go before the gunfight?"

"I didn't know there was going to be a gunfight," I explained. "In fact, I believe I have to go *because* of the gunfight."

"Hold it in, Buttercup. We can't afford to drop our guard."

I did my best to comply.

We soon reached the Nathan Hale Administration Building, which turned out to be the center of campus. Outside, all other buildings radiated around it, like it was the hub of a wheel. Inside, the passage we'd come down funneled into a towering entry hall flanked by sweeping grand staircases. Thick oak doors on one side of the room led outside, while on the other, two significantly larger doors stood open, revealing the school library beyond.

The girl started toward the closest staircase, then suddenly lashed out a hand and clenched my arm. I froze.

She placed her lips a millimeter from my ear and spoke so softly, I almost couldn't hear it. "Two enemy agents.

Upstairs." The words were among the most terrifying I'd ever heard, and yet her warm breath on my ear almost made the danger seem worth it. "I'll have to hold them off. Cut through the library and take the rear stairs up."

"To where?" I tried to be as quiet as her but couldn't. Even my whisper seemed to echo through the room.

On the mezzanine level, a human shape emerged from the shadows.

"The principal's office!" the girl hissed, shoving me forward. "Run!"

I might not have been able to shoot a gun or fight hand to hand, but running, I could handle. I'd had to flee from Dirk Dennett plenty of times. However, I'd never run with a full-on, life-or-death adrenaline surge before. It was like having afterburners. I covered the twenty yards to the library in the blink of an eye.

Gunfire raked the carpet behind me and splintered the doorjamb as I lunged for safety.

The library was cavernous, four floors of wide balconies ringing a central open space. On the main floor was a maze of shelves. Normally, I would have been thrilled by the sheer acres of books, but at the time the library only looked like a gigantic booby trap to me; there were a thousand places for assassins to hide.

In each corner a staircase spiraled up. I zigzagged

through the shelves toward one on the far side of the room and bounded upstairs while the sounds of a gunfight echoed from the entry hall.

A bullet pinged off the banister just as I reached the third floor.

I hit the deck.

On the first floor a black-clad man clutching a machine gun darted toward my staircase.

My Taser wasn't going to do me a damn bit of good from that distance.

But there was a shelf full of reference books nearby.

I snatched the heaviest I could find—*Cooper's Pictorial Guide to Soviet Era Weaponry*—quickly estimated the speed of my attacker in relation to the force of gravity, and determined the exact right moment to drop the book over the railing.

From below came the distinct thud of book colliding with skull, followed by the grunt of the assassin collapsing.

Contrary to everything Mike Brezinski had ever claimed, I had just found a real-world application for algebra.

I dashed up to the fourth floor and found a door that looked as though it hadn't been opened in years. It led to a dingy old stairwell. One more flight up brought me into a long, wide hallway lined with imposing office doors. I dashed down it, scanning the nameplates on each: Dean of Student Affairs; Vice Dean of Risk Assessment; Director of Counterespionage. Finally, in the center, I found a door marked "Principal."

From the direction I'd come, I heard footsteps pounding up the stairs. More than one set.

I threw myself against the principal's door.

It was locked. I bounced off it and landed on my ass in the hall.

There was a computerized keypad to the right of the door, a tiny screen above it reading ENTER ACCESS CODE.

No one had said anything about access codes.

I glanced back toward the dingy stairwell. The footsteps were louder, as though my enemies were almost to the door. They'd emerge within seconds, far too little time for me to race to the safety of the far end of the hall.

The principal's door was the only escape route, and I could think of only one way to get through it.

I flipped on my Taser and jammed it into the keypad. The tiny screen flickered as I shocked the system. Then the electricity overloaded, and every light in the hall blew out, plunging me into darkness.

That had not been my plan.

There was a thump from the end of the hall as an enemy agent banged into the door, followed by what I assumed were curse words in a language I didn't know.

Two seconds later three high-powered flashlight beams flicked on at that end of the hall.

At the opposite end, three more flicked on.

Which meant I was now flanked by six heavily armed men in total darkness.

So I did the only other thing I could think of: I prepared to surrender.

I raised my hands over my head and backed against the principal's door, accidentally bumping the handle.

It lowered with a click.

Apparently, I'd unlocked it.

All six flashlight beams swung toward the sound.

I slipped into the darkened office, slammed the door shut, and promptly ran right into a coffee table. It cut me off at the knees, and I face-planted on the carpet.

The lights snapped on again.

I reflexively tucked myself into a ball and yelled, "Please don't kill me! I don't know anything! I just started here today!"

"Begging for mercy?" said a disappointed voice. "That's D-quality performance for sure."

There were murmurs of assent.

I slowly lifted my eyes from the deep-pile carpet. Instead of a horde of assassins aiming guns at me, I found myself facing a conference table. Two middle-aged men and one middle-aged woman sat on the far side of it, shaking their heads as they jotted notes on legal pads. To the side stood Alexander Hale.

I heard an electronic hum behind me and glanced over my shoulder. There, a bank of monitors presented views of every place I'd been on campus.

I winced as understanding descended. "This was a test?"

"Lucky for you," said the man in the center of the table, the owner of the disappointed voice. He was a stocky man who seemed to think he was more roguish than he truly was. His suit was dotted with food stains, his waistline stretched the fly of his pants to the breaking point, and though his hair was thick and perfectly coiffed, it was also quite obviously a toupee. "If this had been a real incident of external aggression, we'd be mailing your remains home in a doggie bag."

"But I haven't learned anything yet," I countered. "I just got here."

"I'm well aware of that," the man snapped. "The SACSA exam is standard for all students upon arrival."

I looked to Alexander for help.

"Survival and Combat Skills Assessment," he explained, then turned to the panel. "I thought that trick he did with the reference book in the library was rather clever."

"It was a lucky shot," Bad Toupee said dismissively.

"And using the Taser on the keypad?" Alexander asked. "We've never seen that before."

"For good reason. It was moronic." Bad Toupee stood and fixed me with a hard stare. He had a slight tic—a twitch in his left eye—which seemed to be exacerbated by his anger. "I'm the principal of this academy. These are the vice principals, Agents Connor and Dixon. You've already met Alexander Hale . . . and, of course, Erica."

I turned around. The girl was behind me. She had entered without making a sound.

I gave her a half wave hello but got nothing in return.

"I think we're all in agreement that your performance today was deplorable," the principal continued. "You've displayed amateur-level skills or worse in virtually every arena: unarmed combat, elusiveness, savoir faire . . ."

"Is there an essay portion of this test?" I asked hopefully. "I usually do well on those."

The principal glared at me, his left eye twitching wildly. "You're not so hot at knowing when to keep your mouth shut, either. Frankly, if you hadn't done well on your STIQs and shown an extraordinary aptitude for cryptography, I'd be sending you right back home to Mommy and Daddy. But we'll just have to see what we can make of you. You have a lot of work to do, Ripley. And, as of now, a D-minus average."

With that, he waved me away dismissively.

I left the office, feeling hollow inside. I'd never had a grade lower than a B in my life—and that was an 89 in handwriting back in third grade.

I was also slightly confused by something the principal had said. I'd never known I had extraordinary cryptographic ability. In fact, despite my gift for math, I'd always found cryptography rather difficult. Math and logic will get you only so far with many codes; you also need to be good at wordplay. Which was why I could calculate exactly how many seconds I'd been at spy school so far (1,319) but still be stumped by the newspaper's daily jumble on a regular basis.

There had been a few cryptography games on the CIA website. I was under the impression that I'd utterly failed at them, but perhaps they'd been designed to detect some latent skills that even I didn't know about.

Erica stepped into the hall behind me.

"It's nothing to be ashamed of, right?" I asked her. "I mean, I've had no training in *anything* yet. I'll bet no one does well on this test when they first get here."

"I aced it," she told me. And then she left without so much as a good-bye.

Thus, a mere twenty-three minutes after my arrival at spy school, I had learned something extremely important about it: It wasn't going to be easy.

INTIMIDATION

Armistead Dormitory

January 16

1750 hours

Moving from home to a boarding school where I
didn't know anyone would have been difficult under normal
circumstances. After my frightening and humiliating initiation, however, it was traumatic. I was tempted to head right
for the phone to call my parents and ask them to come pick
me up, but then I realized a few things:

1. The SACSA exam was probably *designed* to weed out
people. Being a spy wasn't going to be all good times and
glory. If I couldn't handle a fake life-or-death scenario, how
could I ever be expected to handle a real one?

2. I hadn't made a very good impression on Erica, but if I left, that'd be the *only* impression I'd ever make on her. If I stuck around, I'd at least have a chance to recover.

3. Things couldn't possibly get *worse*. Therefore, they had to get better.

So I decided to stick it out at spy school for at least a little while longer.

Immediately after being dressed down by the principal and blown off by Erica, I found my belongings piled in a slightly damp heap in the hallway outside the office with an orientation packet balanced atop them. Inside was my class schedule, a map of the campus with directions to my room, and a pamphlet detailing emergency procedures for everything ranging from poisoning to nerve gas attacks.

My room was on the top floor of Armistead Dormitory. All first years were sequestered up there. I originally presumed this might be nice, having a room up on top with a view, but this, like 100 percent of my presumptions about spy school, turned out to be wrong. The top floor was basically an attic that had been haphazardly divvied into cramped little rooms. Our dog got more space when we boarded him on vacation.

The walls were thin enough to hear through, and the ceiling, which was really the peaked roof of the building, slanted so precipitously that I could stand upright only in half the room. There was a small dormer window set into the slant, which let in a tiny bit of light and a staggering amount of cold air. Apparently, it had last been weatherproofed during the Kennedy administration. The furniture was army surplus, circa World War II: a spindly cot with a rock-hard mattress, a squat wooden night stand, an iron desk with corners sharp enough to put out an eye, a footlocker, and a folding chair.

There was no personal bathroom. Instead, there was a communal restroom at the far end of the hall with three ancient toilets that made disturbing noises when you flushed them and four showers that appeared to be a breeding ground for rare foot fungi.

There was a small communal lounge at the top of the stairs—a few tattered couches and a yard sale coffee table—but since it was frigid on the floor, no one was hanging out there. I could hear some of my fellow students in their rooms, but none emerged to welcome me to spy school—or even say hello.

While I unpacked in my tiny room, my phone buzzed. It was a text from Mike.

How's loser science school?

It was supposed to be a joke, but it made me feel lousy anyhow. Lousy and lonely.

Awesome.

I wrote back. The great thing about texting is, no one can ever tell when you're lying.

Someone knocked at my door.

I jumped, startled. Most days I probably wouldn't have, but I was a bit skittish after my initiation. I crept to the door and peered through the tiny peephole.

The kid in the hall looked as though he'd stepped off the cover of a glossy magazine. He was several years older than me, well past his awkward teenage phase. He had perfectly coiffed brown hair, a chiseled jaw, and broad shoulders. He wore an expensive sports coat over an even more expensive sweater. If you'd asked me to design the prototypical spy-to-be, I would have drawn *him*. He waved at the peephole knowingly. "Just open the door, Ben. I know you're in there."

I reached for the doorknob, then paused, wondering if this was another test.

"It's not a test," the guy outside the door said. "If I wanted to hurt you, I would've kicked the door in thirty seconds ago. I'm just the welcome wagon."

I opened the door.

The kid breezed in, flashing an acre of teeth as he grinned. "Still shaky after your SACSAs, huh? I get it. I was too. But you've got nothing to worry about from me." He extended a friendly hand. "Chip Schacter. Nice to meet you."

I shook it, pleased to finally meet someone friendly. "Ben Ripley. But I guess you knew that already."

Chip laughed. "Yeah. Every student gets full dossiers on all the new meat. Yours was better than most, though."

"It was?"

"Absolutely. Especially those cryptography scores." Chip whistled appreciatively. "I haven't seen cryptos like that since Chandra Shiksavelli . . . and she went right from here to being a Level 6 at the NSA."

"Wow," I said, trying to seem nonchalant, although I was secretly thrilled. I still wasn't sure how I could be so skilled at cryptography and not know it, but it was nice to finally have some good news. For the first time since I'd arrived at spy school, I actually felt like I might belong there.

"Anyhow," Chip went on, "your first days here can be pretty rough. I figured you could use a friend."

"I could," I admitted. "Thanks."

"I'll take you around, show you the ropes, introduce you to the right people. In a few days you'll have this whole place wired. And all I ask for in return is a little favor."

"That'd be great," I said . . . and then caught myself. "What favor?"

Chip glanced out the door, as though to make sure no one was within earshot, then shut and locked it. "Nothing much. Just a little harmless computer hacking. The kind of thing friends do for each other all the time."

Any enthusiasm I'd had seeped out of me like air from a punctured balloon. "Uh . . . I'm not so good at hacking."

"Doesn't matter. I can walk you through the toughest

stuff. But there's a rotating sixteen-character daisy-chain password protecting the firewall. I can't crack it, but it ought to be a piece of cake for someone with your mad skills." Chip patted me on the shoulder proudly, trying to bolster my ego.

The sad thing is, it sort of worked. I already knew this guy was trouble, and yet, somehow, I still wanted his approval. "What computer would this be?"

"Just the school's mainframe. There's some classified information I need to get off it for a class."

"What kind of information?"

Chip's face clouded. "What's with all the questions? I'm trying to be a friend here, and you're giving me the third degree."

"Sorry, but . . . I just got here. I don't want to do something that's going to get me in trouble."

"You know what'll *really* get you in trouble? Making me an enemy rather than a friend. 'Cause I can be a real good friend . . . or a real *bad* enemy." Chip's muscles tensed, straining the seams of his sports coat.

I gulped. This was unbelievable. At regular school there was one thing I'd been exceptionally good at: avoiding bullies. (The trick was to blend into the crowd and let them pick out prey more obvious than you.) But now I hadn't even made it to my first meal at spy school before one set his sights on me.

Worse, Chip Schacter wasn't like a public school bully.

Those guys were mostly out to cause you embarrassment rather than pain; the worst they might do was yank down your pants while the cheerleading squad was passing. There was something far more menacing about Chip. He was obviously after much more than my lunch money—and the penalty for standing up to him appeared to be pain.

"I don't want to be your enemy," I said, backing up as far as I could in my tiny room.

Chip's muscles relaxed. He flashed a disingenuous smile. "Good to hear. Let's get to it." He ushered me toward the door.

I stayed put. "You want to do this *now*? I haven't even unpacked."

"Exactly. *No one* would ever expect you to do something like this yet. Plus, everyone will be in the dining hall. Dinner starts in five."

"Just out of interest . . . is what we're doing against the rules?"

"There are no rules at spy school."

"So . . . if we get caught . . . ?"

"Ben, I'm your friend, right?"

"Right."

"And friends look out for each other. I'm not gonna let you get caught." Chip clamped a hand on my shoulder and squeezed, sending a shock of pain through my body. "Now, let's stop gabbing like girls and go do this."

He turned to the door, expecting me to follow. I immediately tried to assess what other options I had, but I couldn't come up with any, other than fleeing through the tiny window in my room, which would have merely left me on a steeply slanted, icy roof four stories above the ground.

Going along with Chip didn't seem much safer, however. I already knew not to trust him. If I screwed up hacking the computer—which I was bound to do, as I didn't even know what a rotating sixteen-character daisy-chain password *was*, let alone how to decrypt one—Chip would certainly let me take the fall for it. Which meant I could be bounced from spy school within only hours of arriving.

While I dithered about this, Chip started out the door. As he grabbed the knob, there was a sudden sizzling sound, like that of a steak being dropped on a hot grill. Chip's body went rigid and his hair stood on end while tiny blue bolts of electricity arced between his teeth. He finally managed a grunt of surprise, then collapsed, quivering, on my floor.

The door opened, and a boy about my age with a mop of dark hair draped over one eye peeked in. He prodded Chip with a foot to make sure he was unconscious, then held up a small device that he'd wired to the outside doorknob. "Palm-size Van de Graaff electrostatic generator. Very effective, but only for five minutes. If you want to stay in one piece, I suggest you get far away from here in that time."

INFORMATION

Mess Hall
January 16
1820 hours

"Here's the first thing you need to know about spy school: It sucks."

Murray Hill, the kid who'd rescued me from Chip, crammed another forkful of spaghetti into his mouth. We were in the mess hall, which everyone simply called "the mess," eating dinner. Most of the rest of the student body—three hundred students ranging in age from twelve to eighteen—were gathered in clumps around us. Though no one else had bothered to introduce themselves, everyone was obviously aware of my presence. Every time I glanced toward one of the clumps, I'd catch someone quickly averting their eyes from me.

The mess wasn't terribly far from my room; it was right next to the dormitory. I'd been concerned that it was the first place Chip would come looking for me, but Murray claimed there was safety in numbers. And besides, he was starving.

"Everything you hated about regular school?" Murray went on. "We still have all of that here: rigid social cliques, lousy teachers, incompetent administrators, terrible food, bullies. And on top of that, occasionally, someone tries to kill you."

Murray was thirteen and should have been a second-year student, but he'd been held back after flunking his self-preservation exam the spring before. During the final combat simulation, he'd accidentally shot off the principal's toupee. (They were only using dummy bullets at the time, so the principal was unharmed, but his beloved hairpiece was damaged beyond repair.) Having to repeat his first year didn't seem to bother Murray much, but then, nothing really seemed to bother Murray. Unlike everyone else in the mess, he didn't appear to care how he looked—or what anyone else thought of him. Our fellow students sat ramrod straight and were impeccably dressed, as though concerned that someone might be grading them on their posture and grooming. For the most part, they wore pressed jeans and nice sweaters, clothes that looked professional but would also allow them to move freely in case of a sudden ambush. On the other hand, Murray seemed to be making a deliberate attempt at slovenliness. His hair was unkempt, his shirt was untucked, his sweatshirt was stained a dozen times over—and was currently getting a fresh coat of spaghetti sauce. He had the posture of a piece of wet linguine and his socks didn't match. He was obviously intelligent, though, and when he had something to say—as he did now—he was determined to say it. I was having a hard time getting a word in edgewise.

"Wait," I said. "You mean Chip was trying to—"

"Kill you? No. Then he wouldn't have anyone left to intimidate. What'd he ask you to do?"

"Hack into the school mainframe."

"For what?"

"'Classified information.' For one of his classes."

Murray nodded knowingly. "Test answers, most likely. Chip's tried to force virtually everyone here into helping him cheat one way or another."

"And no one's told the administration?"

"Oh, the administration knows."

"And they haven't kicked him out?"

"This isn't your average school. We're training to be *spies*, not Boy Scouts. You can get an A for cheating here, as long as you do it cleverly enough."

I sat back, trying to make sense of that. "So I *should* have tried to hack the system?"

"Oh, heck no. You'd never have got past the first firewall. The Security Council would've nailed you, Chip would have proclaimed his innocence, and you'd have been sacrificed as a lesson to your fellow students to keep their mitts off the mainframe."

"But you just said cheating was okay—"

"If you do it cleverly enough. Hacking's idiocy."

"But Chip coerced me into it."

"And thus would've kept his hands clean. Doing something stupid isn't so stupid if you can get someone else to do it for you."

I shook my head, dumbstruck by all of this. "That's insanity."

"They don't call this place an institution for nothing. You gonna eat that?"

I looked down at my own plate of spaghetti. It was untouched. After the day's excitement, I didn't have much of an appetite, which wasn't helped by the fact that the food looked disgusting. It's not easy to mess up spaghetti, but somehow, the kitchen staff had managed to do it. The noodles were barely cooked, and the meat sauce looked suspiciously like canned dog food.

I slid my dinner across the table to Murray, who dug

right in. "Big mistake," he told me. "Spaghetti's the best thing they make here. Word to the wise: Stock up on peanut butter and jelly. No one will admit it, but I think they make the food this awful on purpose. They're building up our immunity so that if someone ever tries to poison us, it won't work. Arsenic's got nothing on the meat loaf here."

"Is there *anything* good about this place?" I asked.

Murray waved around the room. "There's a lot of hotness, girl-wise. And some of the classes aren't half bad."

"Like what?"

"The computer stuff's all pretty solid. Good language programs. Oh, and I'd definitely recommend ISEA: Intro to Seducing Enemy Agents. I actually did my homework in that one."

"What about classes in weapons and combat?"

Murray froze, a forkful of spaghetti halfway to his mouth. "Aw, nuts. Don't tell me you're a Fleming."

"What's a Fleming?"

"Someone who comes here actually thinking he's gonna become James Bond."

I got the reference: Ian Fleming had invented James Bond— and thus created several generations of people who naively assumed espionage was a glamorous profession. Like me. I felt my ears reddening slightly in embarrassment, but I tried to play it cool. "This school *is* supposed to teach us how to be spies."

"Yeah. In real life. Which is different from the movies. Hollywood's sold you a false bill of goods, that spying is all tuxedos and nifty gadgets and car chases in awesome places like Monte Carlo and Gstaad. When, really, it's mostly grunt work in third world hellholes like Mogadishu and Newark."

I tried to hide my disappointment. "There must be *some* good assignments. Alexander Hale doesn't look like he's doing much grunt work."

"Yeah, there's maybe one or two cherry jobs. But those are for the cream of the crop. If you want to join the rat race here, busting your butt for the next six years trying to prove yourself, be my guest. But you're not gonna come out on top. *She* is." Murray gestured behind me with his fork.

I knew whom he was pointing at even before I turned around.

I'd noticed Erica the moment I'd come in. She was the only student sitting alone, although her exile appeared self-imposed. Every guy in the mess looked like he wanted to be chatting up Erica; every girl looked like she wished they were friends. But Erica was immune to all of it. She had her nose in a textbook, apparently uninterested in anything—or anyone—else. Given my brief encounter with her, however, I suspected her aloofness was a front; Erica was probably well aware of every single thing going on in the mess at that moment, if not on the entire campus.

"She's the best student here?" I asked. "She doesn't look much older than us."

"She's not. She's only a third year. But technically, she's been at this a lot longer than the rest of us. Seeing as she's a legacy."

I turned back to Murray, about to ask why.

"That's Erica *Hale*," he explained.

Understanding descended on me. "She's Alexander's daughter?!"

"Not to mention granddaughter of Cyrus Hale, great-granddaughter of Obadiah Hale, great-great-granddaughter of Ulysses Hale, and so on. Going all the way back to her great-great-great-great-granddaddy, none other than Nathan Hale himself. Her family's been spying for the United States since before there *was* a United States. If anyone's graduating into the elite forces, it's her."

"So you're not even gonna try?"

Murray shoved his second empty spaghetti bowl aside and dug into dessert, which was green Jell-O with unidentifiable objects suspended in it. "I used to be like you, back when I first got here. I was as gung-ho a Fleming as you've ever seen. But then one day in the middle of my second semester, I'm in the gym here, learning how to fend off an attacker with a machete, when I have this epiphany about becoming a field agent: People try to *kill* field agents. On the other hand, very few people ever try to kill the guys who work at headquarters."

"Hold on," I said. "You *want* a desk job?"

"Absolutely. You work nine to five, get a nice place in the burbs, put in your thirty years, and retire with a big old government pension. Who gives a fig if it's not glamorous? Give me mundane and safe over glamorous and dead any day."

I had to admit, Murray had a point. And yet I still felt that if I worked really hard, someday I could be as good as Erica—and once I was, I'd be very hard to kill.

"Of course, you can't let the administration *think* you want to be a desk jockey." Murray polished off his Jell-O with one long slurp. "They'll bounce you for not being with the program. You've got to make it look good, like you're *trying* to be a field agent, but you just don't quite have the chops. Now, trying to be bad isn't easy . . . although it *is* easier than actually trying to be good."

"Why are you telling me all this?"

"What do you mean?"

I waved around the room at all the clumps of students. "Have you shared this wisdom with everyone else? Why'd you save *me* from Chip?"

"No, I haven't told everyone this," Murray admitted. "Though I've *tried* to tell some, to no avail. As I said, I was like you once. On track to have a miserable school life, followed by a miserable work life. But someone pulled *me* aside and showed me the light. That guy's now a successful desk jockey in the Paris bureau with a hot French girlfriend and a long, happy life ahead of him. I'm merely paying it forward. As for Chip, well . . . simply put, I don't like him. I'll take any excuse I get to render him unconscious. Speaking of which . . ." Murray nodded toward the door.

Chip had entered. He'd taken the time to fix his hair after being electrocuted and was now flanked by two kids even bigger than he was. They were both hulking slabs of muscle with crew cuts and attitudes, though I thought one of them might be a girl.

"Greg Hauser and Kirsten Stubbs," Murray told me. "Neither one's exactly a genius, though the Agency always has use for a few people who are just big and mean and don't question orders."

Everyone in the room paused in mid-conversation to find out whom Chip and his goons were targeting. Every pair of eyes followed him—except Erica's. She stayed riveted to her book, as if unaware anything else was happening.

The other 294 students heaved a collective sigh of relief as they saw Chip, Hauser, and Stubbs heading for Murray and me, not any of them. No one resumed their conversation, though. We were now the center of attention.

Chip slammed a hand on our table so hard that the

plates jumped. "I know you pulled that little stunt earlier," he snarled at Murray.

"I don't know what you're talking about." Murray stayed amazingly calm, given that everyone else in the room seemed to be terrified for his safety. "I was in the computer lab all afternoon, and I have sources to corroborate that."

"Don't give me that garbage!" Chip snapped. "You know exactly what I mean."

"Oh, I'll bet I do," Murray said. "You're referring to the incident where you were trying to intimidate Ben here into helping you cheat because you're not capable of doing your own dirty work, but then you let your guard down and allowed someone to knock you unconscious. Yeah, everyone's talking about it. I can see why you're upset. I'd be embarrassed as heck if I got caught with my pants down like that."

Around the room there were a lot of snickers at Chip's expense, though they were quickly stifled before Hauser and Stubbs could figure out who was making them.

Chip turned crimson in anger. Veins the size of night crawlers bulged in his neck. "You think you're so smart, don't you?"

"Not at all, Chip," Murray replied. "I *know* I'm smart. For example, if I *had* played that little trick on you, I'd have snaked a fiber-optic camera under the door first and recorded the entire event, so that if someone like you or your girlfriends here threatened to retaliate physically, I could threaten to send the video to the principal in return. He might not give a hoot about the coercion or the cheating, but he certainly wouldn't be pleased to see how you got knocked out so easily. That's F-quality self-preservation."

Chip stared at Murray a long time, unsure whether this was a bluff or not, trying to figure out his next move. He ultimately opted for saving face. "But you *didn't* shock me, right?"

"Of course not," Murray replied. "And Ben here had nothing to do with it either."

Chip nodded menacingly. "Well, you let whoever *did* do it know that, one of these days, I'm gonna get the upper hand on him. And when I do, he'll wish he'd never crossed paths with me. Is that clear?"

"Crystal," Murray said.

Chip turned his attention to me. "If I were you, I'd stop hanging out with this loser. It's gonna cause serious harm to any chance you have of a social life here. It might even cause serious harm to *you*."

To emphasize this, Hauser snatched the spoon out of Murray's hand, clenched his fist around it, and squeezed. When he opened his hand again, the steel utensil had been crumpled as though it were a candy wrapper. He plunked it into Murray's milk.

"I'll be keeping my eye on you," Chip warned me. Then he and his thugs stormed off to grab dinner.

"Morons," Murray muttered. "Big muscles. Very little brains. Anyone remotely intelligent would know there wasn't enough time to rig a fiber-optic camera *and* a portable Van de Graaff electrostatic generator. I wouldn't be afraid of them if I were you."

Only, I *was* afraid. In fact, it occurred to me that I'd spent a considerable amount of time since my arrival at spy school in various states of fear, ranging from moderately spooked to completely terrified. In a way, I was even more afraid of Chip than I had been of the enemy agents during my SACSA exam. They'd simply wanted to kill me (or so I'd believed at the time); Chip could make my life miserable for years to come. Given, I'd led a very sheltered life, but up to that point Chip Schacter was the scariest person I'd ever met.

Until that night.

The next guy made Chip look like a cream puff.

ASSASSINATION

Armistead Dormitory
January 17
0130 hours

"Rise and shine, kid."

There are plenty of lousy ways to wake up: having your REM sleep shattered at four a.m. when a raccoon trips your burglar alarm; snapping awake in a boring math class to discover you've been talking about Elizabeth Pasternak in your sleep and everyone has heard it; being pounced on by a young cousin who accidentally drives his knee into your spleen. . . .

But those are all bliss compared to having an assassin jam the barrel of a gun up your nose.

I pried my tired eyes open, saw the man shrouded in black . . . and my primal instincts immediately kicked in.

I leapt into action, springing as far away as I could.

Unfortunately, there was a wall six inches away from me.

I slammed into it hard enough to rattle my teeth, tumbled back into my cot, and found myself right back where I'd started. With the gun pointed at my nose. Only, the assassin was laughing now.

"Man, you should've seen the look on your face," he snorted. "It was classic."

I couldn't tell anything about him in the dark room. A sliver of moonlight through the window illuminated only his gun. He was merely shadow set in deeper shadow.

"Please don't kill me," I said, for the second time that day. It was becoming my mantra.

"Whether I kill you or not is entirely up to you. Let's see how well you play ball."

I wasn't sure how the assassin had gotten into my room. I'd taken the precaution of not only locking the door, but also propping my desk chair underneath the knob—although I'd only thought I was protecting myself from Chip, his goons, or other potential bullies at the time.

After dinner Murray had introduced me to a few fellow students, all of whom had made polite small talk and then run off to do homework. I'd returned to my room to find an inch-thick packet of paperwork to fill out: registration forms, personal skills assessments, applications for false identification, weaponry rental agreements, organ donor cards, and the like. Once I'd finished all that, I'd compared my class schedule with the campus map to figure out everywhere I had to be the next day, logged in to the school computer system to set up my student profile and secure e-mail account, called my parents, lied to them about how great everything was, and discovered, somewhat late, that none of the locks on the toilet stalls in the common restroom worked. Then I'd secured my room—or so I'd thought—read a few pages of a book, and passed out.

According to my alarm clock, it was now one thirty in the morning.

"What do you want?" I asked.

"Tell me about Pinwheel," the assassin replied.

"Pinwheel? What's Pinwheel?"

"You know damn well what it is. Don't play stupid with me!"

"I'm not playing! I really am stupid!" Admittedly, that wasn't the best choice of words, but I was panicked. I was new to having guns aimed at me and might have told my assailant anything I knew to spare my life, but he'd thrown me a major curveball by asking me about something I didn't know anything about. "Are you sure you've got the right guy?"

"You're Benjamin Ripley, aren't you?"

"Uh . . . no." It was worth a shot.

And for half a second it almost seemed to work. The assassin hesitated, slightly confused, then asked, "Then who are you?"

"Jonathan Monkeywarts." I winced. It had been the first name to pop into my head. I made a mental note to be better prepared the next time this happened.

I didn't even see the assassin move in the dark. I only felt it. He snapped my bedsheets so hard that I was catapulted out of bed. I landed hard, whacking my head on the night table. "You think *that's* funny?" he growled. "You think this is all a game?"

"No, I don't." I'd been completely caught off guard by the attack. The room spun around me and sparks of light danced before my eyes. If this guy could cause that much pain using only a sheet, I was terrified what he could do with a gun.

I'd landed on my suitcase, which I hadn't finished unpacking before bed. Its contents had spilled to the floor beneath me. Clothes and books, mostly, though I had a dull sense of something hard digging into my thigh.

"Then let's try this again," the assassin said. "And if you try anything else, I *will* shoot you. What . . . is . . . Pinwheel?"

My pain-clouded brain suddenly realized what the hard

thing was. My tennis racket. The one Alexander Hale had suggested I bring to use as a weapon, just in case. At the time, I'd thought he was making a wry, offhand quip, but now it seemed he'd been eerily prescient.

I grasped the handle, sat up to face the assassin, and tried to stall for time. "Who told you I knew about Pinwheel?"

"What do you think? It's in your file."

That didn't help at all. I didn't have the slightest idea what to say, seeing as there were several million wrong answers that would get me killed. "The thing is . . . it's a . . . well . . ."

"Stop stalling or I'll shoot you."

I had a sudden flash of inspiration. Maybe this guy was after the same thing in my file that had interested Chip. "It has to do with cryptography."

The assassin didn't shoot me, which I took as a good sign. Instead, he snapped, "No kidding it has to do with cryptography. I want to know what it *does*."

I racked my brain, desperately trying to recall my conversation with Chip. "It helps you circumvent a rotating sixteen-character daisy chain."

"Really?" The assassin actually sounded a tiny bit impressed.

"Yes."

"How?"

Nuts. I didn't have the slightest idea how to talk my way

out of this one. But I tried. Maybe if I threw big words at the guy and sounded confident about it, he'd think I was way smarter than he was. "First, you have to set up a quadrilateral subnet matrix, then ossify the syntax and fibrillate the coprolites. . . ."

"Before you say anything else, there's two things you should know," the assassin said. "I'm not an idiot. And I've run out of patience. Don't say I didn't warn you."

Moonlight glinted off the gun as he raised it toward me.

My primal instincts kicked in once again. Only this time, they did a better job.

Before I even knew I was doing it, I'd ducked to the left while bringing the tennis racket around.

It caught the assassin on his wrist, knocking his gun free just as he fired.

I felt the heat of the bullet as it passed over my shoulder and shattered my window.

The gun disappeared into the shadows. We both heard it skitter across the floor and thud into the wall someplace behind me.

I swung the racket wildly, not caring what I hit as long as it was painful. I heard the crack of graphite against bone and the startled yelp of the assassin.

"Help!" I screamed, hopefully loud enough to wake the hall. "Someone's trying to kill—"

The assassin lunged at me before I could finish. My eyes had adjusted enough to the dark room to see things now.

I leapt onto my cot, slipping past him as he tried to land a karate chop, which instead cleaved my bedside table in half. I'd intended to bolt for the door, but my feet got tangled in my sheets and the assassin recovered faster than I'd expected.

He wheeled around, looking to take me down at the knees.

So I bounced on the bed, hacking down with the racket at the same time.

I actually have a great forehand slice. It's the best part of my game. I caught the assassin right above the ear, hard enough to shatter the racket. He gave a gurgle of pain and dropped, bounding off the mattress and landing on the floor with a thud.

I bolted, yanking open the door and racing into the hall. I banged the beheaded racket handle on every door I passed. "Help! Help me! It's an emergency!"

I could hear people groggily waking in their rooms, saw a light flick on from beneath one door. But I didn't stop to wait, fearing I had only temporarily waylaid my assassin. I kept moving for the stairs, screaming the whole way.

I was almost there when the door at the end of the hall opened and my resident adviser emerged. It was the first time we'd met, though my welcome packet had informed me that her name was Tina Cuevo and she was a sixth year. She was tall and beautiful, with jet-black hair and skin the color of hot chocolate. She wore flannel pajamas, bunny slippers, and a look that said she wasn't happy to be roused from her sleep—although this changed to one of astonishment when she saw me.

I wear only underwear when I sleep.

From the moment I'd been attacked, I had been thinking only about how to survive. Now, for the first time, it dawned on me that I was practically naked.

I spun around to find everyone else on the floor emerging from their rooms.

Most of them immediately broke into laughter.

Thankfully, Tina didn't. I think the look of sheer terror on my face convinced her this wasn't a prank. "What's wrong?" she asked.

"There's an assassin in my room. He just tried to kill me."

I'd expected Tina to evacuate the hall and call for help, but that ran counter to her training. Instead, she produced a gun from the pocket of her pajamas—apparently, she slept with it—and went into action mode. "I'll take care of this. There's a robe in my room. For Pete's sake, put it on." She flattened herself against the wall and moved quickly toward my door.

I slipped into her room, which was larger than mine and

far more nicely decorated. There were all sorts of homey touches like framed pictures, window dressings and throw rugs that made me feel oddly safe and secure, given that I'd been running for my life seconds before. The terry-cloth robe hung on a hook by the door. I put it on. It was warm and smelled like cinnamon.

I wasn't sure what to do next. Fleeing still seemed like a perfectly rational option. But it felt wrong to run off in a woman's bathrobe while she was facing an assassin for me. I'd already run down the hall almost nude; I didn't need to make any more faux pas that night. I found a cozy stuffed chair buried under a stack of tutoring manuals and settled into it.

A minute later a fellow student my age poked his head in. "Uh . . . Tina wants to talk to you."

"Where is she?"

"In your room. Duh."

I went back out into the hall. Every doorway now had someone peeking out of it, looking toward me. Heading back to my room seemed like a terrible idea, given that I'd left an assassin in there, but everyone seemed much calmer than they might have if there was still an enemy agent on a killing spree. So I walked back down the gauntlet of gawkers.

Tina emerged from my room as I approached. "About this assassin of yours . . ."

I gulped, concerned. "Did I kill him?"

"That's hard to say." Tina waved me inside. "I'm having a little trouble finding him."

I stepped back into my room. The light was on now. The place was trashed. Furniture was shattered. My belongings were strewn everywhere.

But the assassin was gone.

DEBRIEFING

Armistead Dormitory
January 17
0205 hours

"You're claiming that someone tried to kill you. Tonight."

"You don't believe me?" I asked.

The principal stared at me for a bit. It was hard to tell if he was being careful with his answer or was just sleepy. It was 2:05 in the morning. The principal had been roused only ten minutes before and appeared to be in desperate need of caffeine. As he lived on the school grounds, he had merely wrapped a thick robe over his pajamas and hurried right to the dormitory. His fluffy slippers were soggy from the snow.

"There's no sign of the killer," he said. "Or the weapon."

"He shot through my window," I countered.

"Lots of things could have broken that window."

"There must be a bullet."

"Sure. Somewhere outside under five acres of snow."

I grew exasperated. It probably wasn't the smartest move, but I was tired too. "You really think I trashed my own room and smacked myself around to make it *look* like someone tried to kill me? Why would I do that?"

"I don't know," the principal replied. "To get attention, maybe. The more important question is: Why would someone want to kill *you*? You just started here. You barely passed your SACSAs today. If someone wanted to go to the trouble to get past all our defenses and break into a dormitory to kill someone, you'd think they'd go after somebody *worth* killing."

I paused to think about that. Although the statement was offensive, I had to admit there was some logic to it.

The principal had commandeered Tina's room to question me. My room had been sealed off until a team of expert crime scene investigators could arrive. I hadn't even been allowed to grab my own clothes. I was still wearing Tina's fluffy bathrobe. Together, the principal and I looked like a page from a Bed Bath & Beyond catalog.

There was a knock at the door.

"What is it now?" the principal snapped.

"Thought I might be of service." Alexander Hale slipped inside. Unlike the principal, he was wide awake. In fact, it appeared he hadn't gone to bed yet. He still wore his tuxedo, though the bow tie was undone and the collar was unbuttoned. There was a tiny red smear of what looked like lipstick on his neck. "I came as soon as I heard."

The principal probably would have chewed out anyone else who barged into his interrogation, but he shrank respectfully before Alexander. "Where were you?" he asked.

"Doing a little undercover work at the Russian embassy." Alexander gave a sly wink, then turned to me. "But that's not what's important right now. Are you all right, Benjamin?"

"Yes."

"How'd you escape? Who rescued you?"

"I did it myself."

Alexander whistled appreciatively. "Really? How? Karate? Jujitsu? Krav Maga?"

"Tennis racket."

"Ah! I told you that'd come in handy. Nice work."

The principal shrugged, unimpressed. "It would've been *really* nice if he hadn't allowed the killer to escape."

"It's his first night here," Alexander replied. "He hasn't even had Intro to Self-Defense yet, let alone Enemy Subjugation and Apprehension."

"And yet he fought off a professional assassin? With a mere tennis racket?" the principal asked incredulously. "Maybe there wasn't a killer at all. Maybe it was just some of the older boys hazing him and he couldn't take it."

My thoughts briefly flickered to Chip Schacter. He seemed like a big enough jerk to think threatening someone with a loaded gun was funny.

But then something occurred to me. Something I'd forgotten about in my panic.

"He asked me about something called Pinwheel," I said.

The principal and Alexander both turned toward me, surprised. Then they both tried to hide the fact that they were surprised. Alexander did a considerably better job.

"Pinwheel?" the principal asked, acting as though this was the oddest thing he'd ever heard.

"What is it?" I asked.

"I don't know," the principal replied in a way that suggested he was lying. "I've never heard of it."

"Well, *he* had," I shot back. "He said it was in my file."

The principal and Alexander shared a look. A glimmer of understanding—and perhaps concern—passed between them.

"Benjamin, I'd like you to think about this very carefully," Alexander said. "What, exactly, did the assassin want to know about this Pinwheel?"

I tried to reconstruct the conversation in my room. Even though it hadn't been long before, it wasn't easy to do. My memories of the event were jumbled by fear and adrenaline. "He just wanted to know what it was. I think."

Alexander sat on Tina's bed and looked me in the eye. "And what did you tell him?"

"That I had no idea what it was."

"Are you sure?"

"Yes . . . No, wait. I told him it had something to do with cryptography. But I was only making that up."

"Did he believe it?" the principal asked, intrigued.

"He said he already knew it had to do with cryptography," I answered. "He wanted to know what it *did*. I tried to make something else up, but he knew I was lying and so he tried to kill me."

"Are you sure that's *exactly* what happened?" said Alexander.

"Well, he aimed his gun right at me—," I began.

"But when did he pull the trigger?" Alexander asked. "Before you fought back . . . or after?"

"If I hadn't fought back, he would have killed me," I explained.

Alexander put a hand on my shoulder, signaling me to relax. "Take a moment and think about it. Try to recall everything that happened as it happened. Take your time.

There's no rush. Determining the exact proper sequence of events is important."

I closed my eyes and thought some more. It certainly *seemed* the assassin had been trying to kill me. That was the whole point of being an assassin, after all. But everything had happened so fast—and in the dark, no less. Finally, I had to admit, "I'm not sure if he was trying to shoot me or not. Maybe he was only trying to scare me—and the gun only went off when I hit him with the racket."

Alexander and the principal locked eyes for a moment.

"Does that mean something?" I asked.

"Perhaps. Perhaps not," the principal said, though I could tell he was lying again.

There was another knock at the door.

"What?!" the principal snapped.

A very attractive woman entered. She wore a formfitting pantsuit and, despite being about only thirty, didn't seem fazed by the principal's angry demeanor. Instead, she was all business. "I'm Agent Coloretti, Crime Scene Investigation. I have a preliminary report on the potential assassin."

"It's about time," the principal groused. "What've you got?"

"Nothing," Coloretti responded. "No fingerprints. No blood. Not a single hair left behind."

"So . . . there wasn't an assassin?" the principal asked.

"I didn't say that," Coloretti replied. "Only that there's no concrete evidence of one."

"What about the surveillance cameras in the dormitories?" Alexander asked. "They should have recorded something."

Coloretti sighed. "Yes, they should have . . . if they hadn't been dismantled."

The principal snapped to his feet. "All of them?"

"No, not all of them," Coloretti said. "But enough of them, starting with the ones on the northern perimeter wall about twenty minutes before the incident. Then the ones along the route to the dormitory. And finally, the ones *in* the dormitory. He knew exactly where they all were—and took out every single one that might have recorded him. That, in itself, is evidence that *someone* breached the campus."

"Someone who really knew what he was doing," Alexander added. "Someone professional."

"And yet, not professional enough that he couldn't be beaten by a newbie with a tennis racket," the principal scoffed.

"Perhaps he underestimated his target," Alexander countered. "Everyone does it now and then."

"Really?" the principal asked. "Have you?"

Alexander thought for a bit, then admitted, "No."

Agent Coloretti was staring at me so intently, I checked

to make sure my robe wasn't hanging open. "Given the nature of this event, perhaps the rest of this discussion should be Security Level 4C," she told the others.

Now the principal and Alexander both looked my way as well.

"Yes," the principal agreed. "I think that's well advised."

The three of them started out the door without so much as another word to me.

"Wait!" I said.

They all paused.

"You're just going to leave me here by myself?" I asked. "After someone might have tried to kill me tonight?"

"You saved yourself once," the principal said. "If anyone else comes at you, just do it again."

"But my room's a crime scene," I protested. "Where am I supposed to sleep tonight?"

The principal sighed, as though I were trying to be a constant pain in his rear end. "Where else? In the Box."

DISCLOSURE

The Box
January 17
0500 hours

That's it, I thought, the moment I laid eyes on my new room. *I quit.*

The Box hadn't been designed for use as a dorm room. It had been designed as a holding cell. If I had actually managed to capture my assassin that night, *he* would have ended up in the Box. Instead, I did. Lucky me.

My relocation there wasn't officially a punishment. The Box was simply the safest place for me on campus. It had been designed to keep enemies from getting out—but that also meant it was extremely hard for one's enemies to get *in*.

It was a reinforced cement bunker in the sub-subbasement of the administration building. The walls were three feet thick, and there was a steel door with three separate locks. Outside, it was protected by a matrix of lasers; tripping one would trigger an alarm—and the deployment of sarin nerve gas. There were also seven security cameras, all being monitored in the academy's security command center.

Whereas all this made me safer, it wasn't exactly comfortable. The security staff had made a few token attempts to spruce up the Box for me—a gingham comforter on the bed, a few dog-eared spy novels from the library, a plastic houseplant—but it was still a frigid, windowless block of concrete far removed from any of my fellow students. After a long day of being threatened and humiliated, the Box was the last straw. If it hadn't been the middle of the night, I would have called my parents then and there to ask them to come pick me up and return me to normal life. But I figured I could hunker down and make it to morning. Washing out would be humiliating, and perhaps I'd regret it for the rest of my life, but the rest of my life promised to be much longer if I left spy school.

Even though the Box was the safest place on campus, I couldn't fall asleep. My body was exhausted, but my mind was wired after the night's excitement. Every time I heard a noise, I imagined another assassin was slipping in to kill me.

But beyond that, dozens of questions gnawed at me. What was Pinwheel? How could I have cryptography skills without knowing about them? Why was the principal behaving so strangely? Something mysterious was going on at spy school, and no one was telling me the truth.

I snapped upright in bed for the umpteenth time, thinking I'd heard the door creak. My cheap bedside clock said it was five a.m. I peered into the shadows of the Box, saw nothing, and chided myself for letting my nerves get the best of me yet again.

And then one of the shadows pounced on me.

It hit me full force in the chest, knocking me flat on my cot. The moment I opened my mouth to yell for help, a rag was crammed inside. I brought up my knee, hoping to connect with my assailant's solar plexus, only to find my legs in a scissor lock between theirs.

"Take it easy," my attacker hissed. "I'm not here to hurt you."

If anyone else had said it, I probably wouldn't have believed them, But I recognized the voice. And her smell: lilacs and gunpowder. It was the second time that day I'd been pinioned beneath Erica Hale.

I tried to say I understood, but with the rag in my mouth, it came out as "Mmmmthmmpphffthh." So I relaxed and nodded agreement instead.

"Okay, then," Erica whispered. "I'm going to let you go and take the rag out. But if you make any attempt to fight back or call for help, I *will* hurt you, understand?"

I nodded again.

Erica unscissored her legs and plucked the rag from my mouth.

I reached for my bedside lamp, but she caught my hand. "Don't. There are cameras inside the room. I'd prefer no one know I was here." She sat on the bed, only a foot away, as there was nowhere else for her to go in the tiny room.

As my eyes adjusted to the darkness, she began to take shape. She was sheathed in black, her hair tucked into a black scarf, black commando paint on her face. For a moment, in the extreme quiet, I thought I could hear her heart beating excitedly, but then I realized it was my own.

"How'd you get in here?" I whispered.

"I'm better at breaking and entering than they realize. And I wanted to talk to you."

"About what?"

"What do you think? The assassin. Pinwheel. Something dirty's going on here, and you're in the middle of it."

"Do you know why?"

"Of course I do. Isn't it obvious?"

I toyed with the idea of lying, telling Erica that I wasn't a naive rube, that of course I was aware of what was going on as well, but I knew I wouldn't be able to get away with that for more than thirty seconds and would only end up looking worse. So I went with the truth. "No."

Erica rolled her eyes. "This guy tonight, he came after you because of Pinwheel, right?"

"How'd you know that?"

"I'm studying to be a spy. It's my job to know things."

"Do you know what Pinwheel is?"

"No. But what's really interesting is that *you* don't."

"Why?"

"Because, according to your file, you *invented* it."

I sat upright. "What? That can't be true."

"Exactly."

There was a huge jumbled jigsaw puzzle in my mind, but suddenly, the first two pieces clicked into place. My supposed gift with codes. Pinwheel. *Click. Click.* "Somebody put false information in my file."

"It looks that way."

"Who?"

"Who created your file in the first place?"

"I don't know. Someone in the administration, I guess."

"No. *Lots* of people in the administration: the Admissions Office, Recruitment, Future Student Assessment . . ."

"And one of them inserted false information without the principal knowing?"

Erica gave me a long, hard, disappointed look.

Understanding descended on me. *Click.* "The principal told them to."

"Yes. Though he certainly did it only because someone else told *him* to. He's not exactly Mr. Think-for-Yourself."

"You don't think much of him."

"Ever hear the phrase 'Those who can't do, teach'?"

"Yes."

"Well, the principal can't even teach. The guy's a basket case. Although, in his defense, he's had a bit of a tortured past."

"What happened to him?" I asked.

"He was *tortured*," Erica said. "A lot, in fact. Every time the CIA sent him out into the field, he got captured. He wasn't a very good spy."

"So the CIA put him in charge of the entire spy school?" I asked, incredulous.

"Our government at work." Erica sighed. "The higher-ups probably know he's lousy, though. They just want someone who won't question orders. For example, they've got him fudging your file to deal with the situation here."

"What situation?"

"Your file is supposed to be classified. All documents pertaining to the recruitment of new undercover agents—as well as anything pertaining to the existence of the academy at all—is Security Level A1. For Your Eyes Only, no dissemination allowed. And yet, within eight hours of your arrival here, an enemy agent breaches our perimeter, knowing exactly where to find you and possessing intimate details of your file."

"So . . . there's a mole?" I asked.

"Wow," Erica said sarcastically. "Figured that out already, did you?"

"Who is it?"

"That's the million-dollar question . . . which is where *you* come in."

Click. Another piece of the puzzle fell into place. The reason my file said I had talents I didn't know about was because they didn't exist. "Oh no! I'm the bait?"

I couldn't quite tell in the darkness, but for once, it *looked* like Erica might have been the tiniest bit impressed by my deductive abilities. Which provided only the slimmest comfort, given what I'd just learned. "You got it," she said. "You were brought in as part of Operation Creeping Badger."

"Creeping Badger?" I asked, incredulous.

"I think they're under the impression that badgers hunt moles," Erica explained. "They don't, really, but the guys who named it are spies, not biologists. Anyhow, it appears the plan was to bring you in, make you out to be a big-time crypto whiz boy, and draw out the enemy . . . only the enemy moved a lot faster than the school expected, because the principal and everyone else were caught with their pants down tonight."

My heart was beating even faster, but it wasn't because of Erica now. "The school set me up to have an assassin come after me?!"

"Well, they probably weren't counting on an assassin. But, yes, that's the general idea."

Another puzzle piece clicked into place. Only, the more I saw of the big picture, the less I liked it. "So . . . my recruitment was a sham?"

"Yes."

"Am I even qualified to be a spy?"

"Not really," Erica said. "I think they picked you because you have strong math skills—so on paper, you *look* like you could be a crypto genius. And because you live close by."

I hung my head. There had been a lot of heavy things to deal with today, but this was the heaviest. To go from the euphoria of learning I could be an elite spy to discovering it was all a setup—and one that could have gotten me killed, no less—was devastating. But the more I considered it, the angrier I got.

I thought back to the principal grilling me in Tina's room. "The principal dragged me into this, then acted like *I* was the one who screwed up," I said. "But *he's* the one who dropped the ball. I almost got killed tonight!"

"He probably didn't expect that our perimeter could be breached so easily," Erica said with a sigh. "The idiot. If the enemy knows what's in our top secret files, why wouldn't they know how to get around our security system? This assassin took out every single camera he had to. He knew exactly where they all were. The enemy probably knows more about this campus than the principal does."

"At least your father's involved now," I said. "He won't make any mistakes like that."

To my surprise, rather than agreeing with this, Erica stiffened at the mention of her father. The already-cold temperature in the room seemed to drop a few degrees. "Yes. Alexander's involved," she said noncommittally.

It seemed best to try to change the subject. "He spent a lot of time trying to get me to figure out the sequence of what happened in my room. Why?"

"To assess who the enemy might be. We know almost nothing about them, other than that they have access to our information. So here's how the mole hunt works: They bring in a patsy—that'd be you—*who* they make out to be an amazing new recruit, a prodigy at cracking codes. This makes you a game changer. Not only is all their coded material at risk now, but you've invented something—code-named Pinwheel— that's going to change everything as far as cryptography is concerned. Pinwheel is what we call a 'hook.' They don't specify what it is, only that it's revolutionary, to get the enemy interested. Then they sit back and wait for the enemy to show.

"Now, what the enemy does with this information tells us something about them. If they simply try to kill you, they're thugs. They perceive you as a threat and they want to eliminate you. But if they try to coerce you into explaining Pinwheel to them, that's a different story."

"That's what this guy was trying to do. Scare me into telling him about it."

Erica nodded. "Whoever we're up against is smart. They want what you know. Or, at least, what they *think* you know. The good news is, you're probably worth more to them alive than dead."

"And the bad news is, this isn't the last time someone's going to come for me."

"Right. Though they won't do it the same way next time. They've played that hand already."

"Do you have any idea who we're talking about here?" I asked. "Who are these people?"

"Oh, there's lots of possibilities: criminal organizations, multinational corporations looking to protect their interests, disgruntled former agents with a bone to pick . . . though I'd say the good money's on a rival agency from another country. One that views America and the CIA as a threat."

"Why do you say that?"

"It makes sense, given what they did here last time."

"Wait. This isn't the first time they've infiltrated the school?"

Erica studied me for a moment, assessing how much she could share. "Didn't you think it was odd, being recruited to a new school in the middle of January?"

"Yes. I asked your father about it."

"And what'd he say?"

"There was a sudden opening." The moment the words left my mouth, I realized that they, like so many other things I'd heard at spy school, were a euphemism for a much darker story. "Oh no! Someone got killed?"

"Joshua Hallal. A sixth year. Incredibly talented. Would've been top of his class, one of the best undercover agents the academy has ever produced, a real threat to our enemies." Erica turned away. I couldn't tell for sure, but it looked as though there might have been a tear in her eye. Which would have been the first trace of emotion I'd seen her display. "The school covered it up, of course. Claimed Josh had a virulent allergic reaction to a bee sting. Which made him unfit to serve, so they rotated him out and placed him and his family in the Witness Protection Program. They might as well have just told us that they sent him to a farm upstate where there's lots of room for him to run."

"What really happened to him?"

Erica shrugged. "I don't know the details . . . yet. All I know is that it happened. And it scared everyone from the school administration on up to the president himself. No one outside of the academy should have known who Josh was. Not even his parents."

I frowned.

"What?" Erica asked.

"There must be a lot of good future spies here," I said. "Maybe not all as good as you and Joshua. But close. Why'd they go through so much trouble to kill *him*? Especially when it revealed that they have a mole inside."

Erica looked back at me. I thought I saw the tiniest trace of a smile bend the corners of her mouth. "You might suck at being a spy right now, but you're not stupid. You're right. It was risky for them to take out Josh. Which means there was probably a reason they did it."

"Any ideas?"

"I'm working on it."

"Are you supposed to be?"

"No. The administration is, but they've pretty much botched things royally so far. Your little visit tonight being exhibit A. This could've all ended tonight if they'd let me be involved. Or *anyone* competent, really. It's a shame. Josh deserves better. So let's just consider this a covert extra-credit assignment for us right now."

I felt a flush of excitement. "Us?"

"You think I've gone through all the trouble to sneak in here and spill my guts to you for fun? Number one mistake the administration has made so far: not letting you know you're the patsy. True, they probably figured you'd freak out and hit the bricks, but still . . . that's no way to run an operation. Ours is going to be a lot better. We're going to uncover this mole, find out who he works for, and take the whole thing down. Are you with me?"

Erica held out her hand. I glanced at it warily.

It was obvious that my plan to leave for home in the morning was no longer valid. There were agents for an unknown enemy organization looking for me; and if they were willing to infiltrate a well-guarded, top secret campus to get me, our neighborhood patrol probably wasn't going to keep me safe. I'd be better off at spy school than anywhere else.

However, that belief had little to do with the administration—which had screwed up pretty much everything they'd touched—and a lot to do with Erica. And though Erica seemed to have some qualms about her father being involved, I didn't. In fact, I was happy to have Alexander Hale on the case.

But agreeing to a covert investigation was another thing entirely. It was reckless, dangerous, insubordinate—and daunting, given that I hadn't taken a single espionage class yet.

On the other hand, it'd give me an excuse to spend time with Erica. Most likely, the only excuse I'd ever have. If I turned her down, she'd probably never deign to speak to me again.

And yet there was something else that motivated me even more than my schoolboy crush: the chance to prove myself.

The academy had only recruited me as bait, for my math and my proximity. They didn't think I had what it took to be a spy, and thus, chances were that, once the mole hunt was over, they'd find a way to jettison me. However, if I helped find the mole, that'd *prove* I was CIA material. They couldn't get rid of me then.

Plus, even though it was dangerous, it seemed less dangerous than waiting around for the administration to take care of things.

In the end, however, it was really the getting-to-hang-out-with-Erica thing that made up my mind.

I shook her hand. It was soft and warm.

"What do we do next?" I asked.

DISSEMINATION

Hammond Quadrangle

January 17

0850 hours

"Hey, Ben," Mike said. **"How's your lame science**
school?"

I should have ignored the phone call. It was 8:50 a.m.
and I was trying to figure out how to get to my first class.
But after all that had happened, I was desperate to hear a
friendly voice.

"It's not lame," I countered. "In fact, it's been pretty
exciting."

"Sure it has. What'd you do last night? Homework?"

"Not exactly."

"Want to know what I did? Hung out with Elizabeth Pasternak."

My step faltered in surprise. "You did not!"

"I did so."

"When?"

"After my older brother's hockey game. Her brother's on his team. Our families all went out for ice cream afterward. We sat right next to each other. She even let me share her sundae."

"Oh." I squinted at my campus map as it flapped in the wind. It was bitterly cold. Two inches of fresh snow had already turned to slush on the campus walkways.

"And get this," Mike went on. "Her parents are letting her have some friends over tomorrow night. Guess who's invited?"

"No way."

"No need to sound so down. She said I could bring a friend. Maybe my brother could bring me by and we could spring you."

"I don't think that'll work," I sighed. I'd been expecting Mike to tell me about a boring night in front of the TV, something that would make my new life sound infinitely cooler. Instead, I was missing out on the social opportunity of a lifetime.

"Are you crazy? You're gonna pass on a Pasternak party?"

"It's not like she'd talk to us anyhow."

"Of course she would! And all her friends are gonna be there: Chloe Carter, Ashley Dinero, Frances Davidson. . . . You can't pass on something like this! Do they even *have* girls at science school?"

"There's lots of girls here."

"Yeah. Science dork girls."

"No. Hot girls. In fact, there's one—Erica—who makes Elizabeth Pasternak look like my aunt Mitzi."

"Liar."

"I'm serious. Next time I see her, I'll send you a picture."

"Go right ahead. And don't think you can send me some photo of a model from a catalog or something, because I can tell."

"She's real, Mike. And she's unbelievable."

Out of the corner of my eye, I noticed a clump of fellow students cloaked in heavy jackets and winter boots. Instead of walking to class like everyone else, they were watching me. But when I turned their way, they all quickly averted their eyes and pretended to be looking somewhere else.

"Okay," Mike said, giving in. "So there's one hot girl. She'll never hang out with you."

"She did last night."

There was a slight pause before Mike responded. When he did, I could sense something in his voice I'd never heard before: jealousy. "In a communal coed dorm sort of situation, right? Like in *Harry Potter*?"

"No. My own room. She came to see me. After curfew. And she went through a lot of trouble to do it."

I was probably violating about twelve security directives by sharing this, but I couldn't help myself. Besides, I wasn't sharing the entire truth about the school. Only the good stuff.

"What'd you do?" Mike asked. It was like I'd hooked a fish.

"Just talked. For a *really* long time."

"About what?"

"She wants me to work on a project with her. Just the two of us."

"What kind of project? Some kind of smarty-pants science thing?"

"It's a little more interesting than that. I'm gonna be spending a *lot* of time with her."

"Wow. Sounds awesome."

"It is. I have to go. I'm late for class." I wasn't saying that just to leave him hanging, wanting more. I was really in danger of being late. I fell in with a group of students as they shoved through the doors of Bushnell Hall.

"Send me that photo!"

"Okay. Bye." I pocketed my phone with a smile. It was time to begin my training.

NINJAS

Bushnell Hall
Lecture Room 2C
January 17
0930 hours

My first class was Introduction to Self-Preservation.
I'd have been excited about it even if I *didn't* think it would
come in handy, given my recent circumstances. I was expecting a quick immersion into hand-to-hand combat or perhaps
a scintillating discussion of how to incapacitate an armed
man.

Instead, it was a snore. Two minutes into the first lecture,
I was already nodding off.

This was partly because I'd had no sleep the night before,

but mostly because Professor Lucas Crandall had the charisma of a rock. Crandall was quite old, with unkempt white hair, the stooped posture of a question mark, and eyebrows that looked as though they'd recently been in a tornado. He was rumored to have served the CIA from the very early days, and he appeared to have been shunted off to spy school because no one had the heart to fire him. He rambled in a wheezing voice that was almost impossible to hear, often losing his train of thought and then pausing for great swaths of time to remember what he'd been saying.

Thank goodness Murray had saved a seat for me in the back row.

Class was in a large lecture hall, like on a college campus, rather than the type of small, boxy classroom I was used to from normal school. A tiered semicircle of seats faced a podium and blackboard. I'd entered late, having lost my way in the building, though thankfully, class hadn't begun, as Crandall was late as well. My fellow students had shrewdly filled all the back rows, leaving the front rows a desert of open seats. I'd reluctantly started down to them when Murray yelled, "Ripley! Over here!"

He yanked his backpack off a back row seat and waved me over. "Never *ever* sit in the front row in a class here," he warned. "Even if it means getting here early."

"Why not?"

"Depends on the class. In Psychological Warfare, Miss Farnsworth has nasty halitosis. In Arms and Armaments, there's shrapnel. In this one . . . well, it's soporific. Crandall doesn't appreciate seeing students passed out in the front row. Luckily, he can't see much beyond that."

Crandall had shuffled in shortly afterward, looking startled to find an entire lecture hall staring at him, as though perhaps he'd forgotten what he was coming to do. He spent the next three minutes searching his pockets for his notes and the two minutes after that searching for his reading glasses, after which he finally got around to the lecture, which wasn't nearly as stimulating as I'd hoped. Crandall wasn't the worst teacher I'd ever had—that'd have been Mr. Cochran, my fifth-grade history teacher, who hadn't known when the War of 1812 took place—but his lecture style was dry as dust.

The general idea behind Intro to Self-Preservation turned out to be that the best way to stay alive was to not get into situations where you could be killed in the first place. This made sense in theory, but it wasn't particularly helpful when you had assassins threatening to drop by your room on a regular basis. This morning's lecture was on how to avoid ninjas, which might have been interesting if step one hadn't been "Stay out of Japan." Furthermore, Crandall had quickly become sidetracked, relating a rambling tale from his own Cold War days.

The next thing I knew, Murray was shaking me awake. "If you're gonna snooze, try these," he said, slipping something into my hand.

It was a pair of cheap glasses, though he'd cut out the eyes from a magazine photo and pasted them over the lenses. While I'd been unconscious, he'd slipped a similar pair on himself. They were ineffective and disconcerting at close range, but you could see how, to someone lecturing eighty feet away, you'd appear wide-eyed and rapt with attention, even while sound asleep.

"Thanks." I accepted the glasses, though I didn't put them on yet. I *wanted* to stay awake; it just wasn't going to be easy. I tried to shake the cobwebs out of my head.

"Don't fight it," Murray said. "If we could weaponize Crandall's lectures, we'd never have to worry about our enemies ever again. We could just bore them to death."

Normally, I wouldn't have pursued a conversation during a lecture, but half the class was doing it while Crandall droned on, completely unaware he was being ignored. "Didn't you flunk this class last year?" I asked.

"Twice," Murray replied.

"Don't you think you should try staying awake through it this time?"

"Sure, if I were going to be a field agent. But the best way to avoid that is to be a guy who can't even pass Self-

Preservation 101. The Administration's going to be so worried about me that they'll assign me to the safest desk job in the Agency. Probably won't even let me use a stapler. Plus, I kind of like repeating this class. I can catch up on my sleep." With that, Murray slumped in his seat, rested his head against the back wall, and shut his eyes.

I tried to focus on Crandall's lecture, but he'd veered off topic again and was blathering on about how much he'd hated the borscht in Russia. So I turned my attention to my surroundings, as Erica had ordered me to.

She'd laid out a plan for me in the Box the night before: "For right now there's two parts," she'd said. "First, we figure out who had access to your file."

"It seems like *everyone* did," I'd replied. "Everyone knew about Pinwheel. You, the assassin, Chip Schacter . . ."

"That's only three people. There's three hundred students at the school, fifty faculty, and seventy-five support staff." Then she frowned. "Chip knew?"

"He showed up at my room right after I did, wanting me to hack into the mainframe for him."

"Let me guess. To fudge his test scores."

"Yes."

"Wow. He's an even bigger idiot than I thought."

"Why?"

"You ever see those movies where some computer

specialist hacks into any site they want in less than a minute?"

"Sure."

"Total nonsense. The CIA has hacking specialists, and it can take them *months* to crack a mainframe. Then they take everything they know and use it to protect ours. Which means the CIA's mainframe is virtually impossible to hack. And yet Chip thinks that just because you know something about codes, you can do it."

"But the fact that he knew about my cryptographic abilities means *something*, doesn't it?"

"I suppose. It'd be worth finding out how he got his hands on your file."

"How did *you*?"

"How'd my father know so much about you when he came to recruit you?"

I nodded, understanding. "He was given a copy."

"A dossier, yes. He didn't keep a very good eye on it."

"Wait. He was given a *physical* copy of my file? This isn't all computerized?"

"At the Computer Illiterate Agency? Not exactly."

"But you said there's a mainframe."

"That doesn't mean everyone knows how to use it. Your file was probably written on a computer and stored on the mainframe. But then it was disseminated to various people to assess your fit for Creeping Badger. A lot of these guys are old school: terrified that someone will hack their e-mail but perfectly happy to leave a top secret dossier lying around their house. Hard copies got printed out . . . and one of them ended up in the hands of the mole."

"So who was sent a copy besides your father?"

"I don't know. The identities of the review panel members are classified. To find them, we'll have to hack the mainframe."

"What? You just said that was impossible."

"No. I said it was *virtually* impossible. Nothing's completely impossible."

"So how do we do it?"

"Take advantage of the weakest link in the computer's protection system. The human one."

"You really *enjoy* being cryptic, don't you?" I asked.

Erica gave me a hard look. "I'm still working on the details. In the meanwhile, you can work on part two of our plan: Keep your eyes open."

"For what?"

"Anything of interest. *Everything* of interest. We know the mole knows who you are and is keeping an eye on you. So let's try to catch them at it. If anyone's following you, I want to know. If they're watching you—or pretending like they're *not* watching you—I want to know. Anything out of the ordinary happens, I want to know."

"I just got here. As far as I'm concerned, *everything* that happens is out of the ordinary."

"Okay, anything *really* out of the ordinary, then. Just be alert."

So I did my best. I stayed as alert as possible for someone who'd weathered two attempts on his life the day before (one imagined, but still, it *felt* real enough at the time) and hadn't managed a wink of sleep all night. The problem was, it was more difficult than I'd expected to tell who was paying attention to me . . .

Because *the whole school* was paying attention to me.

They were trying to act like they weren't, but they were. Not just the clump of students I'd spied outside the building on the way to class. There'd been other clumps in the mess that morning and a gaggle in the hall on the way to class . . . and now, as I studied the class from the last row, there were an awful lot of students with their necks torqued around, studying me right back.

The girl sitting on the other side of Murray from me didn't even try to hide it. She couldn't at such close range. She was a fellow first year, still wearing her naiveté like a badge, so thin that her winter jacket seemed to swallow her, but with green eyes so bright and big that she looked like a cartoon character. "You're Ben Ripley, right?" she asked. "The guy who fought off an assassin last night?"

The way she said it actually made me sound pretty cool. I had to stifle a smile. "Uh . . . yeah. That's me."

"Awesome." The girl seemed legitimately excited to meet me. "Is that why they recruited you last minute? Because you're some sort of martial arts expert?"

"No," I admitted. "I'm really just good at math."

"Right," the girl said. "Coding and stuff. Everyone's heard that. But it's a smoke screen, right? Because Adam Zarembok's a coding expert, and that guy can't even fight off a mosquito. Meanwhile, there's seniors *majoring* in martial arts here who haven't defeated an assassin."

"Well, none of them have ever been *attacked* by an assassin," a weaselly boy sitting in the row in front of us countered. Now that the green-eyed girl had begun talking to me, everyone within earshot had turned their attention my way, blatantly ignoring Professor Crandall.

"I know," Green Eyes said, then looked back to me and asked, "So why have *you*?"

"It wasn't a real attack. It was part of my SACSAs." I hated to lie, but Erica had warned me not let anyone know of the mole hunt.

"No it wasn't. SACSAs are never run at night," the weaselly kid announced. "And the word is, you tanked yours."

"Or *faked* tanking them," the green-eyed girl snapped, coming to my defense. "To make any assassins *think* you couldn't defeat them. Which you then did. So, really, what was that all about?"

"Hey!" Murray chided, not even opening his eyes. "Let the guy be, will ya? Some of us are trying to sleep here."

This didn't deter anyone. More and more students were looking my way.

"I'm not at liberty to say," I told them. It was all I could think of.

A lot of people frowned, disappointed.

"Of course you're not," the girl said, then extended a thin hand that was dwarfed by the sleeve of her jacket. "I'm Zoe. I think what you did was incredible."

In my whole life I'd never had a girl introduce herself to me, let alone say that anything I had done was incredible. It felt good. So did having so many people impressed by me, whether I deserved it or not. Only a few hours before, I'd been mortified, embarrassed, frightened, and depressed by everything that had transpired at spy school. But for the time being, I'd gone from being a nobody to someone of interest.

"It's nice to meet you." I shook Zoe's hand across Murray's lap.

"Nice hands," Zoe said. "Can you kill with them?"

"I haven't tried yet," I admitted, and Zoe giggled.

"I'm Warren," the weaselly kid interjected. He didn't seem to appreciate the fact that Zoe was giggling at something I'd said.

Several other of my fellow first years introduced themselves as well. I did my best to commit them and the faces they went with to memory. Dashiell, Violet, Coco, Marni, Buster, and a pair of Kiras . . .

"You're all pathetic," someone down the row snapped.

I leaned forward to see who it was—and found Greg Hauser, Chip Schacter's mess hall goon, glaring back at me. "*He's* a loser, and you're all double losers for thinking he's not."

"He kicked an assassin's ass last night," Zoe shot back. "While you've flunked this class how many times? Four so far?"

Hauser's giant brow furrowed deep enough to plant corn in. "Last night was all a fake. Chip told me. I mean, *look* at him." He stabbed a meaty finger toward me. "He's a dork. If that had been a *real* assassin, he'd be dead."

"If it was a fake, why'd the administration go to DEF-CON 4 last night?" Zoe asked. "The principal was freaking out in his bunny slippers. Face it, Ben's the real deal. He could mop the floor with you."

"Maybe he and I should put that to the test, then," Hauser said. "In the gym, after lunch today."

"You're on," said Zoe.

"Wait," I said. Once again, I'd been stunned by how fast things could take a turn for the worse at spy school. "I don't think that's such a good idea."

"Why?" Hauser taunted. "You chicken?"

"Of course he's not," Zoe sneered.

Word that there might be a fight quickly rippled through the room. Now virtually the entire class was staring at me.

I looked to Murray, hopeful he might know how to get me out of this predicament. He was asleep. With his fake-eye glasses on, he appeared to be the only person still paying attention to the lecture.

So I tried my best to wing an answer. "I'd just prefer not to. I fought an assassin last night. I think I ought to rest up today."

"Mr. Ripley!" Crandall snapped.

All eyes, including mine, turned back toward the podium.

Crandall had finally regained his focus—and turned it all on me. His unruly white eyebrows dipped over angry eyes. "You're new here, aren't you?"

"Uh . . . yes."

"Did you transfer here from a school where it was acceptable to hold court during a professor's lecture?" Crandall asked.

"No, sir," I replied.

"Ah. Then am I to presume from your ignorance of my lecture that you feel you have nothing more to learn about the art of self-preservation?"

The other students quickly shifted away from me. Zoe acted as though she'd had nothing to do with the conversation. Even Hauser feigned innocence.

"No, sir," I repeated.

"Then it must just be today's topic that bores you," Crandall said. "I'm assuming you've read last night's assignment, chapters 64 to 67 in Stern's *Basics of Self-Preservation*?"

I hadn't even been issued my books yet. It was something I'd planned on asking the professor about at the end of class. "Uh—well—," I stammered. "I think there's been a mistake."

"Perhaps," Crandall said coolly. "Let's see. Why don't we test your knowledge with a little pop quiz?"

The moment he said these words, every one of my fellow students went wide-eyed with fear. And then they evacuated the room. The seats around me cleared out as though I'd suddenly turned poisonous. Even Murray snapped awake and bolted. "Nice knowing you," he said.

Within seconds, the lecture hall was empty except for Crandall and me.

"What kind of a pop quiz is this?" I asked nervously.

"One on today's topic: ninjas." Crandall opened a door by the podium and three ninjas vaulted through. They were clad in black from head to toe and armed to the teeth.

You've got to be kidding, I thought. And then I bolted toward the exit. The doors automatically locked as I approached. My fellow students peered through the windows in them, watching with a mixture of concern and relief that it wasn't *them* inside the room.

A throwing star embedded in the door. I spun to find the ninjas creeping slowly up the steps. The one in front spun a pair of razor-sharp sai knives. The other two twirled nunchucks. Crandall watched from the podium, already frowning at my performance. "Rule number one for fighting ninjas: *Never* turn your back on them," he clucked.

I held my backpack in front of me. I didn't think it would do much in the way of defense, but it was all I had. "Can I just take an F for this?" I asked. "I'm very sorry for talking during class. I'll never do it again!"

"Let's see what he's made of," Crandall said.

The ninjas whooped loud enough to shake the room and charged.

I threw my backpack at them. The first sliced it in half in midair.

I ran. I went straight down the aisle between seats, thinking that this school was even crazier than I could have ever imagined, praying that this was merely another fake-out, that they wouldn't ever really *hurt* a student. . . .

Something whistled through the air behind me.

I turned to find a nunchuck quickly closing the gap between the ninja who'd thrown it and my forehead.

This was followed by an absolutely incredible amount of pain.

And then everything went black.

ALLIANCE

The Eagle's Nest
January 17
2000 hours

"Finally! The young agent awakes!"

I groaned. My head felt like it had been filled with rocks and then rolled down a hill. Even opening my eyes to the light hurt, though it was marginally preferable to going back to sleep again: The last few hours had been filled with nightmares of ninjas and assassins.

My first glimpse of my surroundings seemed light-years away from spy school. So far, everything I'd encountered at the academy had been cold and hard: industrial shades of gray and Cold War décor. But the room I lay in was warm and cozy. The walls were hung with hunting prints and lined with shelves full of leather-bound books. A fire crackled in a large stone fireplace. I was sprawled on a couch that was wonderfully soft and smelled like a pine forest.

Alexander Hale popped into view, swaddled in a burgundy smoking jacket and sipping a glass of neon green Gatorade. "How's the noggin?"

"It hurts," I said. My forehead right between my eyes was the worst. I touched it gingerly and found a lump the size of a robin's egg.

"Don't I know it. I remember the first time *I* was attacked by ninjas. North Korea. I'd only graduated from the academy a few months before. My martial arts skills weren't what they are now, but thankfully, there were only two of them and I had an exploding belt buckle." Alexander stared into the fire wistfully. "Ah, memories."

I sat up, grimacing, glanced toward the window . . . and found, to my shock, that it was dark outside. "What time is it?"

"Dinner-ish. You've been out all day."

"All day?! Shouldn't I be in a hospital?"

Alexander chuckled. "For a little bump? This was nothing. Once, in Afghanistan, I was unconscious for eight days. Besides, you seemed like you needed the rest. How about some Gatorade?"

"Uh, sure."

"Coming right up." Alexander ducked into a small kitchen and opened the refrigerator. It was full of mineral water and various hues of Gatorade. "Proper hydration is extremely important in our business. Although you don't want to overdo it either. I once had to urinate so badly during a gunfight in Venice that I lost focus and almost took a bullet to the brain. What flavor? Glacier Freeze? Riptide Rush?"

"Orange."

"Ah. A traditionalist. Very good." Alexander poured a tall, chilled glass and brought it to me.

He was right. It *did* make me feel better. The ache in my head subsided and my mind was clearing, although I still felt a bit fuzzy around the edges. For instance, I knew there was something wrong about the room we were in, but I couldn't put my finger on what.

"Where am I?" I asked.

"You're still on campus. There *was* some discussion of taking you to the infirmary, but given your precarious situation vis-à-vis enemy agents, I felt it'd be safer to keep you here, in my personal quarters."

"You mean . . . you *live* on campus?"

Alexander laughed heartily. "Heavens no. I have a real home in the city. This is more of a pied-à-terre—for those times when work dictates that I need to be here. And right now I need to be here."

"To help hunt for the mole."

Alexander's eyebrows arched. It was the first time I'd ever seen him off guard. Which meant he had no idea Erica had come to see me the night before; for some reason, she hadn't told him. I wondered why this might be—and if I'd made a mistake mentioning the mole hunt at all.

Thankfully, Alexander didn't get suspicious. Instead, he seemed pleased. "Figured it out on your own, did you? I *told* them you were smart. How'd you put it all together?"

If Erica wanted her investigation to remain a secret, I decided to keep it a secret. "Well, when I considered my fake cryptography skills, the assassination attempt, and the principal's reaction to it, it all seemed kind of obvious."

Alexander laughed again, then slapped my knee and plopped himself into an overstuffed chair nearby. "To you, perhaps. But it wouldn't have to everyone. Good work, Ben. You remind me of myself when I was younger. A real self-starter. When I was only twenty-two, I tracked down an arms dealer in Djakarta who had eluded the DEA for a decade. Well, now that the wool's off your eyes, I think you might be of service."

"I thought the principal wanted to keep me in the dark about all this."

"And as far as he knows, you'll be there. In fact, no one has to know you're helping me but me."

"Not even Erica?"

Once again, Alexander seemed slightly thrown, as though he wasn't quite sure what to say about his daughter for a few moments. "Erica's an excellent student. I admit, I've given her quite a bit of tutoring on the side over the years. She's going to be an incredible agent someday. . . . But I'm not sure she's ready for this."

"And *I* am?"

"Well, you don't really have a choice in the matter, do you? You're a part of it whether you want to be or not. I think it'd be best if we keep this between us for now. It'll be our little clandestine operation. You must be starving."

He said this last bit quickly, as though he was trying to change the subject. But he was right. I hadn't eaten since breakfast. "I am."

"I have some frozen dinners. Not exactly filet mignon, but it's still better than anything you'll get down in the mess." Alexander sprang back into the kitchenette and rooted through the freezer. "Pizza okay?"

"That'd be great, thanks."

Alexander dug out a pepperoni one and tossed it in the oven. "All right, let's get down to brass tacks. Any idea as to who the mole might be?"

"Um . . . ," I said. "I was hoping *you'd* know that."

"Oh, I have my suspicions," Alexander said. "But I only decided to enter the fray today. You've been in the thick of this. Ergo, your thoughts matter. So . . . what do you think?"

"I don't know. I haven't really had much time to investigate . . . and I've been unconscious most of the day. . . ."

"Yes, but you must have some idea. A gut instinct?"

"Chip Schacter."

"Aha!" Alexander perched on the edge of his chair, eyes wide with excitement. "And why do you suspect him?"

"He knew what was in my file very early on. I'd barely been in my room a minute before he showed up, wanting me to hack into the school mainframe for him."

"To steal secrets?"

"No. To alter his grades."

"Or so he claimed," Alexander said suspiciously. "Decent cover story. I assume he threatened you with force?"

"Yes."

"So you hack in, he steals the files, and if anything goes wrong, you get burned. Clever."

Erica's assessment of Chip from the night before came back to me. "But Chip isn't really known for being clever, is he?"

"No, but that could all be a ruse. He could be *so* clever, he's extremely good at appearing not clever at all. After all, he was smart enough to get into the academy, wasn't he?"

That was true. Whereas I'd only been accepted for my potential as bait. Which meant that, on some level, Chip was better spy material than me, no matter what Erica thought of him. "I guess."

"So he has classified knowledge about you, and he quickly tries to use your skills for nefarious purposes. Anything else suspicious about him?"

"Well . . . I didn't do what he wanted . . . and he wasn't happy about that. So he threatened me." I suddenly realized something. "And then, that very night, the assassin came to my room."

"Interesting." Alexander remained calm and collected, but his eyes were alive with excitement. "Might be Chip turning the screws on you."

"Yes! And then, by this morning, he was spreading rumors that the assassination attempt was a fake."

"A campaign of disinformation. Very clever indeed. I think Mr. Schacter has definite mole potential. Good work, my boy." Alexander patted my knee, then headed back into the kitchen to check on the pizza.

I couldn't help but smile. Alexander Hale, one of the greatest spies in America, wasn't only proposing that we run a clandestine operation together; he was also pleased with my investigative skills. His odd relationship with Erica—

the fact that neither wanted the other to know what they were up to—nagged at me a bit, but I could certainly understand both their motives. Alexander was trying to protect his daughter from danger, while Erica was trying to prove she could be an agent without help from her father. I didn't like keeping secrets from either of them, but it did give me an opportunity to work with both the master spy and his beautiful daughter. It was almost enough to make up for the downside: that someone might try to kill me soon.

Alexander slid the warm pizza onto a chopping block. There was an umbrella stand full of bladed weapons nearby. He selected a cavalry sword and hacked the pizza into eighths. "Any other possible suspects rattling around that brain of yours?"

I thought a bit. Another name popped into my head. "I don't know about this one, but you said to trust my feelings. . . ."

"Never question your instincts. Once, I was headed to a safe house in Qatar when I had a sense something was wrong. No evidence at all, just my gut. So I didn't go in. Thirty seconds later the place exploded. Nawaz-al-Jazzirrah had infiltrated the place and rigged it with enough C4 explosive to sink a battleship. If I hadn't trusted myself, I'd be a fine mist right now. So, what's your gut telling you?"

"Well, if it's conceivable that Chip could be playing

dumb, then why not one of his goons, who are supposedly even dumber than he is?"

"Now you're talking. Whom do you suspect?" Alexander slid the pizza onto the mahogany coffee table in front of me. He'd left it in the oven too long and burned the crust, but I didn't care. I was famished.

"Greg Hauser," I said between bites. "He was the one who got me in trouble in Professor Crandall's class today. He *claimed* Chip said the assassin was a fake, but what if Chip never said that? Maybe it was Hauser's idea all along, and he's shifting the blame to Chip. In fact, maybe Hauser put Chip up to trying to bully me into hacking the mainframe in the first place."

Alexander chewed his pizza thoughtfully. "Hmmm. The old Petersburg Puppeteer . . ."

"What?"

"Oh, sorry. Just a little bit of espionage lingo. It refers to someone who *looks* like he's merely the henchman, but really, he's the criminal mastermind, pulling all the strings. Often, the puppet doesn't even know he's being used. We call it the Petersburg Puppeteer after an infamous Cold War Russian operative who looked like a lowly pencil pusher at the St. Petersburg KGB, but who turned out to be running the show. I like this Hauser lead. I like it a lot."

Alexander's cell phone rang. He checked the caller ID. "Oh. I have to take this. It's a contact."

He quickly slipped into the bedroom, leaving me to polish off my pizza by the fire. He didn't close the door, though, so I could hear faint snippets of his conversation:

"Where should we meet? . . . Ah, very good. I love the opera. . . . Of course I'll use an alias. . . . That soon? . . . All right."

He returned two minutes later, smartly dressed in a tuxedo. "Duty calls, I'm afraid. But we've done excellent work here today. Truly excellent. How was the pizza?"

"Great," I lied.

Alexander fastened his cuff links. "Sorry, but I need to blindfold you before we leave. The location of these quarters is classified."

"Oh. All right." It occurred to me that I hadn't left the couch the whole time I'd been there. I hadn't even glanced out the window. So I had no idea where Alexander's quarters were in relation to any other building on campus.

My jacket and snow boots were right by the couch. I tugged them on. "So what do we do now?"

"*You* simply keep doing what you've been doing. Keep a close eye on Schacter and Hauser—and anyone else you find suspicious. I'll see what I can dig up on them. I've got quite a lot of experience with moles. Uncovered one in Karachi just last year." Alexander cinched a wool scarf over my eyes, plunging me into darkness. "Can you see anything?"

"No."

"Perfect."

There was a metallic clank, then the sound of something large sliding open. I finally realized what had been odd about Alexander's quarters: There wasn't a front door.

Not an obvious one, anyway. I assumed the entrance was hidden behind one of the many bookshelves. We stepped into what I could tell was an elevator, though I couldn't guess how many floors it went down. A blast of cold air hit us when the doors opened again.

Alexander led me through a few more twists and turns, possibly doubling back once or twice, before yanking off the blindfold. We were in the grand entry hall of the Hale Building. Outside, fresh snow was collecting on the windshield of Alexander's Porsche.

"Stay alert!" Alexander told me. "I'll be in touch!" Then he wrapped the scarf around his neck and headed out into the cold.

It was only as he drove away that I realized one more odd thing about that night:

While I'd given Alexander all the leads I had, he hadn't shared a single piece of information about his investigation with me. Not one.

WAR

Academy Training Grounds
February 8
1400 hours

"Die, Ripley!" My attacker sprang from behind a rock, blasting her gun indiscriminately.

I fled through the woods, ammo exploding off the trees around me.

I didn't know my attacker's name, though I recognized her from Chemistry 102: Poisons and Explosives. She was a year older than me, mousy and reserved in class, though out here, on the field of battle, she'd found a way to release her inner Rambo.

Of course she knew me. *Everyone* knew me already. I'd

been at spy school for only three weeks, but I was famous, either as the kid who'd outfought an assassin with a tennis racket—or the kid who'd gotten creamed by a ninja in record time in his first class.

I came to a snowy slope that plunged steeply toward a creek and dove onto it. A paintball whistled past my ear and splattered a rock. The snow had been at the academy as long as I had; a crust of icy rime had formed atop it, making the slope a luge run. I careened down it headfirst, leaving my attacker behind but quickly picking up speed.

At the bottom, straight ahead of me, sat a pile of jagged rocks.

The idea of a combat simulation had been appealing at first. So far, classes at spy school had proved a disappointment. As Murray had warned, they weren't much different than classes at regular school: boring. Primary Investigative Techniques was mind-numbingly dull. History of American Spying was really just American history with a few spy stories thrown in; it should have been interesting, but our instructor, Professor Weeks, had taught it so many times that she seemed to be falling asleep during her own lectures. Algebra—and its uses in calibrating one's aim—might have been challenging if I wasn't gifted in it; Professor Jacobi said I ought to be bumped up to calculus, but the paperwork hadn't gone through yet. And after the excitement of my pop quiz, Crandall's self-preservation lectures had slipped back into a series of doddering reminiscences.

A war game promised a chance to get outside and have some fun. We were basically going to be playing capture the flag with paintball guns. I hadn't expected to stay alive very long; I figured I'd just run around in the trees a bit, get ambushed, and then retire to the "morgue" for a hot chocolate with the other corpses. But then the weather turned out to be frigid and sleeting. And Coach Macauley, our PE teacher, announced that our grade would be dictated by how long we stayed alive. The first quarter of the class to die would get D's.

Nobody wanted a D except Murray, who "accidentally" shot himself in the stomach thirty seconds into the game and went off to take a nap.

The rocks at the bottom of the gully were coming up fast. I jammed the butt of my gun into the ice and hung on hard. The gun jolted to a stop and I whipped around it. I kept sliding, moving fast enough to yank the gun back out of the snow, but now I was at least sliding feetfirst. I slammed into the rocks with the soles of my snow boots rather than my face.

My attacker appeared at the top of the hill, gun at the ready. She leveled it toward me.

I tried to swing mine into position, but the strap had got

tangled around my arm during the slide. I struggled to get my gloved fingers around the trigger.

The girl had me right in her sights. "Nice knowing ya," she smirked.

And then a red paintball nailed her in the helmet, splattering all over her face guard.

For a brief moment I was impressed with myself, amazed I'd somehow managed to fire off a kill shot.

Then I realized I hadn't.

Zoe popped out from the jagged rocks behind me, cradling her paintball gun. "Little lesson for you!" she shouted at the girl she'd just downed. "Save the snarky comments for *after* you've killed your opponent!"

The dead girl stuck her tongue out at us, then trudged off to the morgue.

I got to my feet, shaking snow out of my jacket. I was about to say thanks, but Zoe beat me to it.

"Nice work there, Smokescreen. Led her right to me. How'd you even know I was hiding down here?"

I considered telling the truth: I'd had no idea Zoe was hiding behind the rocks. She'd saved my bacon. But I didn't. Without Zoe, I might have been the lamest kid on campus. Instead, thanks to her, I was Smokescreen.

Zoe was big into nicknames. And despite all the evidence to the contrary, she thought I was cool. After witnessing my quick defeat by the ninjas, she'd proclaimed to anyone who'd listen that I'd merely faked the loss. It was a smoke screen: a ruse to convince my enemies that I had no skills, when, in reality, I was a lean, mean killing machine. According to Zoe, I'd done the same thing on my SACSAs, which had led the assassin who came to my room later that night to think I'd be easy prey. In fact, Zoe publicly presumed that I'd actually killed the assassin and that the school had covered it up. She was so supportive that even my embarrassing loss to the ninjas bolstered her belief in me: No one could have really lost a fight that quickly, she insisted. It was such an awful display of self-defense, it *had* to be fake.

Although Zoe was only a first year like me, she was very persuasive. The story rapidly gained a life of its own. Chip and his goons, Hauser and Stubbs, did their best to push their own version of the story: I had no idea what I was doing and had simply got lucky against the assassin, which was pretty much the truth. But since not many people liked or trusted Chip, this only served to give Zoe's version of the story more credence. The school was now divided into two camps. The majority thought I was Smokescreen, some kind of covert superspy who occasionally pretended to be inept. The rest suspected I actually *was* inept. I wasn't exactly comfortable with so many people believing a lie about me, but it was still far better than everyone knowing the truth. The past three weeks had been far easier than my first day; I'd even managed to make a few friends and have some fun. The downside was, I knew it would last only so long. It was only a matter of time before everyone found out the truth; this was a school full of potential spies, after all. So I figured I might as well keep the ride going as long as possible.

"I've been keeping tabs on everyone's position," I told Zoe, who looked at me with wide-eyed wonder.

The main thing I'd learned in my time at spy school was this: *Everyone* there was impressive. I'd been spoiled at my old school. There hadn't been much competition for top student; I think my math teacher had stopped bothering to even grade my tests and begun rubber-stamping them with A's.

Meanwhile, the students at spy school were the cream of the crop from around the country. They were brilliant. They were athletic. They were awe-inspiring. There were students who could defeat ten ninjas at once, students who could take out snipers while riding a horse, students who could build bombs out of household objects and chewing gum, and at least two who'd mastered piloting a helicopter while fighting an assailant with a knife (at least on the simulator). I'd begun to understand why my math skills alone hadn't been enough for me to make the cut.

But I was still determined to prove I belonged there.

As tedious as the classes were, I'd thrown myself into my studies, tearing through my textbooks, trying to learn everything I could. (I was still sleeping in the Box, and though it wasn't pretty, the solitary confinement made it easy to study without distractions.) I put in extra time at the gym and the shooting range.

And then something like the war game would come along, proving that I still had light-years to go to catch up with my fellow students.

Zoe and I ducked into a hollow in the jagged rocks where she'd been hiding until I'd come along. "What's the plan, Smokescreen?" she asked.

I had no idea what the plan was. The best I had was to hide in the rocks and wait for everyone else to kill one another off, which I knew wouldn't go over well with Zoe or our instructors. However, I'd learned one valuable lesson from Alexander Hale: You could always get someone who respected you to do your thinking for you.

"I'm still assessing the options," I said. "What're you working on?"

"Trying to find the flag," Zoe replied. "Chameleon's out doing recon."

A dove cooed close by, which was odd, given that they'd all gone south for the winter.

Zoe cooed back. "Here he is now."

Warren slipped into our small cave. I wasn't a big fan of his—he was peevish and had a big chip on his shoulder—but it was undeniable that he was an expert at camouflage. He'd used tree sap to gum large chunks of moss and tree bark all over him, then blackened his face with dirt. There were even a few snails perched on him for good measure. He looked like a walking terrarium.

Warren was momentarily startled to see me, then seemed caught between relief and annoyance. I'd already determined that he had a crush on Zoe—he followed her around like an enemy agent—and he didn't like how much attention she gave me. On the other hand, he'd bought her stories about my skills hook, line, and sinker.

"Good news," Zoe said. "Smokescreen's teaming up with us!"

"Awesome," Warren said flatly.

"What'd you find?" I asked.

"The blue team has their flag up on the roof of the old mill." Warren sketched a map in the dirt with a stick. "There's five men guarding, four at the corners, and Bull's-eye's up on the roof."

Zoe frowned. Bull's-eye Bailey was the best sniper in the school, a fifth year who was rumored to be able to decapitate a flea with a bullet from a mile away. "That's gonna be tough."

"No kidding," Warren groused. "He took out three members of our team while I was watching."

Zoe and Warren looked to me expectantly.

"I've never been to the mill," I said. "Can you give me a breakdown?"

I hadn't had time to see a lot of the campus. Given that I had potential assassins looking for me, wandering the grounds alone didn't seem like such a hot idea. Besides, any time I hadn't spent studying or training, I'd spent trying to help track down the mole.

Unfortunately, I hadn't got far with that, either. Whenever I got close to Chip or Hauser, they'd seemed as intent on watching me as I was on watching them. Neither had done anything suspicious. I hadn't found any other possible moles either. The only time I'd thought I had a lead was when I spotted Oleg Kolsky, a third year, covertly slipping off the campus. I'd immediately texted Erica, who'd gone after him—only to find he was making an unauthorized trip to the arcade.

Erica hadn't made any more visits to my room, mostly staying in touch with me by somehow slipping notes into my new book bag. (Campus had provided me with an official academy bag after the ninjas had demolished my old one.) I had no idea how she did it. One day I'd tried to keep my bag in sight all afternoon, and there'd still been a note in it afterward. Her messages generally instructed me to leave my updates on various pieces of paper secreted around campus, which was embarrassing because I never had anything to report. Other than this, Erica showed no sign she knew I was alive, let alone collaborating on a mission with her. This was no different than the treatment she gave everyone else, though. She just sat by herself, always studying, immune to anyone else's presence. Zoe called her Ice Queen.

Still, that was more contact than I'd had with Alexander, who seemed to have vanished from existence. I hadn't heard squat from him.

"The mill's built into the side of a hill by a stream toward the back of the property," Zoe explained. "It's been there since the Civil War. Big old stony thing. Probably the best way to attack is to come around the back and approach from up the hill." She looked at me expectantly.

I imagined what Alexander would have said to me. "Good thinking. Let's go with that. What else?"

Zoe beamed, actually thankful I'd praised her. Warren tried his best not to look sullen and failed.

"We'll probably need a distraction to get Bull's-eye's attention," Zoe suggested. "Chameleon, that's you."

Now Warren made no attempt to hide his sullenness. "Me? Why can't I go after the flag?"

"Do you know how to take out a sniper?" Zoe asked.

"No," Warren replied.

"Well, there you go," Zoe said.

Unfortunately, I had no idea how to take out a sniper either. But I couldn't tell *them* that. "How do we access the roof? Can we scale the walls?"

Zoe grinned proudly, then produced a grappling hook from her backpack. "I assume you know how to use this?" she asked.

I didn't. I'd never even *seen* a grappling hook until that moment. Not outside of the movies. I couldn't even imagine where she'd got it. I'd never noticed a grappling hook store— or a grappling hook section at Target—in my life. "Uh . . . I've never used this particular model before," I covered. "I've only worked with the German ones."

"Oh." Zoe seemed embarrassed. "I don't know how those work."

"Then maybe you should work it," I said. "I trust you."

Zoe beamed again. Warren looked like he wanted to brain me with a rock.

"Let's move," I said, even though I would have been happy to stay in our little nook in the rocks all day. It was out of the wind and the sleet, and with all of us crammed in there, it was almost warm. But I had a reputation to keep.

We set out into the cold, working our way up the icy streambed, keeping low, listening to the sounds of battle in the distance. The fight had been going on for over an hour now; I had to assume we'd remained alive long enough to get C's.

We synchronized our watches, then split up by a large oak tree around a bend from the old mill. Warren stayed where he was, curling up and tucking a sheet of moss over him so that he looked like a log. Zoe and I set out to loop around up the hill so we could approach the mill from behind. Birdcalls—or any vocalizations—were no longer an option for communication; the other team would see right through that. So the plan was simply that, in exactly half an hour, Warren would start a diversion. Then Zoe and I would use the grappling hook to scale the mill, take out Bull's-eye and the other guards, and recover the flag.

The whole time, I had a secret plan, which was that somehow, in the next half hour, someone else from our team would come up with a better plan, wipe out the blue team, and win the game. But it didn't seem likely. As we looped around, we noticed many members of the opposing team in the distance . . . and found quite a lot of evidence of our own team members' deaths—usually splatters of blue paint surrounding imprints of bodies in the snow. We didn't say a thing, moving slowly and quietly.

After twenty-five minutes we'd crested the hill and had the mill in sight. The flag was still there; no one else had beat us to it. Around the mill the four guards were starting to get cold and bored. The two at the corners closest to us had left their posts and were chatting about something. Up on the roof, though, Bull's-eye was still on alert, sweeping the horizon with his gun.

"You'll have to take him out from here," Zoe told me.

I'd been afraid she'd say that. She was right. It was our best chance to get him, and we wouldn't stand a chance of recovering the flag if he was still alive. But I was still having trouble hitting a silhouette twenty feet away on the shooting range, let alone a live human 140 yards away in a sleet storm. I could instantly *calculate* where I had to aim to make the shot, but it took an entirely different set of skills to hold the gun perfectly steady and fire it. One major way movies differ from real life is that, in real life, guns are *heavy*. Aiming them is extremely difficult. Plus, with every shot, they kick back hard enough to bruise you, which means you have to aim again every time you fire. In the movies every hero seems to be able to hit an enemy right between the eyes, even when the enemy is at the far end of a football field, surrounded by innocent hostages, and the hero is dangling by one hand from a runaway helicopter. In real life even a crack shot like Bull's-eye couldn't pull that off.

On the other hand, if I fired at Bull's-eye and missed— which was a very likely scenario—he stood a decent chance of being able to shoot me before I could regain my aim and hit him. Thus, shooting at him seemed like a very bad idea; but if I pawned off one more job on Zoe, she'd start to suspect I had no idea what I was doing.

"All right," I said, setting up my gun. "But this isn't going to be easy. I'm more of a hand-to-hand combat kind of guy."

"I know," she said. "That's why you'll have to lead the attack once you've taken Bull's-eye out."

Me and my big mouth, I thought.

I set my gun in the crook of a tree, steadying it, then checked my watch. It was two minutes until Warren was due to create his diversion. Bull's-eye would theoretically be distracted, and I'd theoretically take him out.

Zoe took out the telescopic range finder to coordinate my aim.

A twig snapped to our left.

It was far away, but the wind had stopped blowing for once and the sound carried.

Zoe and I turned that way, fearing an ambush.

Instead, we saw two members of the enemy team in the distance. They'd frozen in mid-step, aware they'd made a telltale noise and were looking around to see if anyone had heard. They were fifty yards away, too far to make out their faces.

We were hunkered down close to the base of the tree, hopefully blending in with it.

"Do they see us?" I whispered, barely loud enough to hear.

"I can't tell. Check it out." Zoe handed me the scope. I was in a better position to see our opponents than she was.

I put it to my eye with as little movement as possible. The scope worked like a digital zoom camera lens, automatically focusing on the others so I could instantly see who they were.

"It's Chip and Hauser," I said.

They didn't see us. After a few seconds they seemed convinced no one had heard them and continued walking. Only, they weren't coming toward the mill or heading toward where our flag was hidden. Instead, they slunk toward the back wall of the property, away from the war game altogether. They were taking great care to not be noticed.

"Looks like they're not after us," Zoe said with a sigh. Then she checked her watch. "T minus sixty seconds to diversion."

She held out her hand for the scope, but I didn't return it to her. I kept watching Chip and Hauser.

It seemed like they were up to something. If they were, the timing was right. The entire student body and faculty were focused on the war, but no one was keeping tabs on where anyone specific was at any exact time.

"Smokescreen!" Zoe hissed. "They're unimportant. Gimme the scope!"

"Sorry. Something's going on here." I racked the focus on the scope, trying to see where they were heading. A small stone shed by the back fence sprang into view.

"T minus forty!" Zoe said. "We're gonna blow the game!"

"This is more important," I told her.

"C'mon, it's only Chip," she argued. "Chameleon's about to martyr himself here!"

Chip and Hauser reached the shed. Chip reached into his pocket. . . .

A war whoop echoed from down the hill, past the mill.

It was Warren. Thirty seconds early. Apparently, we hadn't synchronized our watches right.

Chip and Hauser turned toward the sound, startled.

"Nuts!" Zoe snatched the scope from my hand and spun it toward the mill.

I could barely see Chip and Hauser through the sleet without the scope.

I turned to grab it back, and as I did, I caught a glimpse of the disaster unfolding down the hill. A log had suddenly sprung to life and was charging headlong toward the mill, firing its gun indiscriminately. Warren.

The blue team guards all turned his way. Even Bull's-eye was distracted.

I fired my gun at him, hoping for the best . . .

And pegged a tree ten feet away, missing my target by a mere 130 yards.

The guards and Bull's-eye all opened fire at once upon Warren. He would have been an easy target, even for me. So many blue paintballs smeared him that, within three seconds, he looked like a Smurf.

As this happened, something burst out of the snow on our side of the mill, away from the action. It took me a moment to realize it was a person. Someone who'd somehow dug through the snow to within mere feet of the guards without them noticing. The person hit the mill wall running and scrambled up it like a squirrel, no grappling hook required.

"It's Erica!" Zoe crowed, watching through the scope.

I'd already guessed. It couldn't have been anyone else. But I grabbed the scope back to see her anyway.

Within seconds, she was atop the mill. Bull's-eye was dead before he even knew she was there.

Other blue team members, ones we hadn't even noticed, emerged from the woods around the mill, racing toward it to stop the inevitable. They opened fire on Erica, but it was too late. She'd already snatched the flag.

Everyone's attention was on the mill.

Except that of two people, I guessed.

I took off in the direction I'd last seen Chip. Erica's attack had taken only a few seconds, but I'd allowed myself to be distracted by it for too long.

I darted through trees and leapt rocks, skidding on ice and snow, until I reached the stone shed. Two sets of footprints led through the snow to the door, which was still propped open, thanks to a clod of ice that had got in the way.

I hesitated, unsure whether to yank the door open and surprise Chip and Hauser, but then the wind took care of the decision for me. It blew the door wide open.

The shed was only a few feet square, gardening implements piled several deep around the walls.

There was no sign of Chip and Hauser inside.

They'd vanished into thin air.

SURVEILLANCE

Sublevel 1
February 8
1445 hours

Although a lot of surprising things occurred at spy school, I was relatively sure no one there was capable of instantaneous molecular dispersion. I knew Chip and Hauser had come into the shed: Their wet boot prints still marked the floor. The trick was to figure out where they'd gone.

I was wary of going after them myself, given that both of them were significantly bigger than me and had several years more training in how to cause serious pain in other people. But there wasn't much choice. In the distance I could see my team's victory celebration had already begun. Zoe and everyone else were racing toward the mill, chanting Erica's name. It would take several minutes for me to go back and convince anyone to come help me, minutes I didn't have if I wanted to stay close to Chip and Hauser.

But beneath my concern, there was a current of excitement as well. Outside, everyone else was merely pretending to be spies, while I had been given the opportunity to actually be one. I had an honest-to-God mission: to find out what Chip was up to. And if I did it right, people might soon be chanting *my* name.

I cased the shed for clues. It was freestanding, which meant there was only one direction Chip and Hauser could have gone: down.

I looked at the floor again. It was weathered concrete, chipped and scarred from years of poor treatment. There was a small square of it in the center of the shed, three feet on each side, nested inside a larger square that made up the rest of the floor. Chip's and Hauser's boot prints were confined to the central square, except for one. This was a toe print on the far side from the door, as though one of them had been reaching for something high up.

I quickly examined the far wall. A rack of garden tools hung from it—hoes, rakes, shovels, hedge clippers—with rusty blades and well-worn handles. It was like I'd stepped into a gardening catalog in 1950. Above that was a second rack holding smaller items: lanterns, trowels, loops of extension cord. The toe print seemed angled toward a trowel. As both Chip and Hauser were at least six inches taller than me, I had to clamber onto a sack of fertilizer to reach it.

The trowel was welded to its rusty hook, so it didn't come off. Instead, it swiveled upward when I grabbed it, like a light switch.

There was a soft metallic click from inside the wall, followed by a loud hiss from under the shed. The inner square of concrete suddenly lowered into the floor.

I pulled the shed door shut and leapt onto the square.

It sank into a subterranean tunnel thirty feet below the surface. The tunnel was fifteen feet wide and ten feet tall, big enough to drive a golf cart through. The walls, ceiling, and floor were all cement. Tree roots had forced their way through cracks in the ceiling, meaning the tunnel had been around for decades. Water dripped through the cracks, puddling on the floor, giving the whole place a dank, mildewy smell, like the showers in our middle school gym.

The tunnel was well lit—lights studded the ceiling every few feet—though it curved as it headed back toward the school, so I couldn't see anyone ahead. I could *hear* them, though. Chip and Hauser weren't bothering to whisper, confident no one knew they were there, and their voices echoed back to me.

I hopped off the cement square. The tunnel dead-ended behind it, right where the wall of the academy property would be. There were two red buttons with up and down arrows on the wall nearby, like those you'd find in an elevator. I pushed the up one.

The concrete square rose back up, allowing me to see how it worked. A pneumatic column lifted it, silent except for the hiss of air, quiet enough that Chip and Hauser didn't hear it over their own voices. The concrete square slotted back perfectly into the ceiling above.

Fearing my heavy snow boots would be loud on the cement floor, I yanked them off and carried them, padding down the hall in my socks. Once I rounded the curve, I could see Chip and Hauser in the distance, moving quickly, as though with a purpose.

They weren't talking about anything clandestine. Hauser was just going on about how unfair Professor Oxley's last offensive driving exam had been. "We had to drive these ancient cars with manual transmissions. When was the last time anyone even saw a car with a manual transmission?"

"Gotta be prepared for anything," Chip said.

"Well, it wasn't just me who couldn't do it," Hauser snapped defensively. "Stubbs didn't even know how to get hers out of first gear. Finally, she jammed the thing into reverse and nearly took out half the class."

As we got closer to the heart of the campus, more tunnels began to branch off the one we were in. And then doors began to appear in them. The first I passed had a plate on it: B-213–STORAGE. The next read B-212, also storage. Soon the place became a labyrinth. We hooked left and right through it. If I hadn't had my targets in sight, I would have lost them. And I doubted I could find my way back to the shed, though I figured that wasn't problematic. We'd entered what was obviously an important subterranean level of the campus. The shed, with its small pneumatic lift, couldn't have been the only entrance. There had to be other ways in and out.

Still, I was astounded by the size of the underground level—and that I'd had no idea it was there. It occurred to me that Alexander had said something right before my SACSA exam began about there being "far more here than meets the eye," but at the time I'd thought he was merely being metaphoric. For the last three weeks I'd assumed the buildings I saw aboveground made up the entire campus. Now I realized that, as with so many other things at spy school, there was far more going on beneath the surface.

We began to pass other rooms, rooms that housed mechanical and electrical equipment, secretive unmarked rooms with multiple key-code entries, dormitories and mess halls that probably dated back to the Cold War, when everyone feared a nuclear war might force them to live underground for a year. Pipes and electrical wires snaked along the walls and ceiling. Random objects, like filing cabinets and hand trucks, began to appear in the halls, as though despite all the storage rooms, there still hadn't been enough places to put them. Throughout, it was all eerily unpopulated; everyone was still outside.

However, that was likely to change soon, now that the war was over—and Chip knew it. He kept glancing at his watch and hustling Hauser onward.

Then he suddenly stopped. They were in a nondescript section of tunnel that looked exactly like every other section of tunnel we'd been through.

I ducked behind a cart loaded with sacks of powdered eggs just as Chip furtively glanced in my direction. He didn't see me—or anyone else—and decided the coast was clear.

"Check it out," he whispered, then pointed to something nestled among some pipes along the wall.

"Holy cow," gasped Hauser.

I was still carrying Zoe's scope. I put it to my eye and zoomed in. I caught a glimpse of a nest of red and blue wires and some yellowish putty before Hauser shifted on his feet and blocked it from view.

I couldn't be sure, but it *looked* like a bomb. Of course, I only knew about bombs from the movies. I'd never seen one in real life. (Explosive Construction and Defusion didn't get taught until our fourth year, when our eye-hand coordination was a bit steadier.) For all I knew, a *real* bomb looked like a sprig of posies.

"Got the kit?" Chip asked.

Hauser pulled a small gray box out of his pocket, though once again, I couldn't see what they were doing with it. Hauser was a big guy to begin with; wearing his bulky winter clothes, he blocked half the tunnel.

"So this is Scorpius, huh?" Hauser asked.

"*Scorpio,*" Chip corrected. "Hold that steady."

Hauser shifted to the side. I caught a glimpse of the wires again.

If I wanted Erica or Alexander to believe this, I needed evidence. I fished my cell phone out of my pocket and pressed the camera to the scopes's eyepiece, thinking maybe I could use it as a telephoto lens. It was hard to hold both pieces of equipment steady, though, so I rested the scope atop a sack of powdered eggs and tried to focus it.

My phone suddenly vibrated in my hand.

It was a text. I'd tried to use my phone underground hundreds of times in Washington—virtually every time I'd ridden the subway—and never once had I got reception. But now, in a subterranean hall thirty feet below ground level, my phone had chosen to work at the least opportune moment possible. The unexpected vibration startled me. I bumped the scope, which rolled off the sack and clattered to the floor.

And if that hadn't been loud enough in the otherwise silent tunnel, the scope noisily rolled away from me—and right toward Chip and Hauser.

There was no use hiding anymore. I ran.

"Hey!" Chip yelled. Then I heard his footsteps and Hauser's pounding down the hall behind me.

I ducked around the first corner I came to, hoping they hadn't seen my face, then took the next corner as well. I tried to look for landmarks so I'd be able to find my way back to the bomb later, but every hall looked the same and I was moving too fast to read the numbers on the doors.

I spotted a staircase ahead and charged toward it, though my stocking feet couldn't get much purchase on the slick floor. I heard the footsteps bearing down on me from behind.

"Might as well stop, Ripley!" Chip taunted. "You can run, but you can't hide! I'll find you sooner or later!"

Later still seemed like the better option to me. I charged up the stairs. Two flights up was a steel door. I hit it with everything I had . . .

Just as Chip caught up to me. He snagged the hood of my snow jacket, though my inertia pulled him forward too. We tumbled onto a well-worn carpet.

I rolled over to find Chip's fist on a collision course with my face. I dodged to the right. Chip's knuckles grazed my earlobe, then connected with the floor.

While Chip howled in pain, I tried to scramble away, but he caught my ankle and yanked my feet out from under me.

"What'd you see?" he demanded.

"Nothing!" I kicked his arm with my free foot, trying to wriggle loose.

Chip pounced on me.

In the movies, when spies fight, they always look very cool, using a combination of martial arts moves and cleverly improvised weapons, often in an incredibly picturesque location, like a castle in the French Alps.

This fight wasn't anything like that. Chip certainly knew how to fight—it turned out that the one area he really excelled in was martial arts—whereas I'd barely had any training at all. However, I'd spent just about any spare time I had in the past few weeks boning up on self-defense techniques. Given the circumstances, I went with a move called the "Bashful Armadillo," which simply involved curling myself into a ball and covering my head with my arms. I chose this for two reasons: (1) It was ridiculously easy, and thus I had already mastered it, as opposed to far more complicated procedures like the "Wily Chipmunk" or the "Spastic Cobra"; and (2) I was wearing thick winter clothes, which not only insulated me from the cold, but also from Chip's attacks.

Chip was therefore reduced to fighting on my level, tumbling around on the floor with me and trying to get a shot in. He landed a few punches on my arms and torso, but my ski parka was so well padded, he might have been hitting me with a throw pillow. Meanwhile, I went for pressure points, trying to get him to release me—an eye gouge or a knee to the testicles—though the best I managed was to drive my elbow into a chair.

"Oh, for Pete's sake!" Chip snarled. "Would you just fight like a man?"

"I'll pass," I said. The Bashful Armadillo was working for me.

"What is going on here?!"

The principal's voice was frightening enough to scare even Chip cold. Our fight stopped instantly.

For the first time since emerging from the subterranean level, I had a chance to take in my surroundings. I'd spent the entire battle with my head under my arms. It turned out, we'd emerged inside the main hall of the Hale Building— from behind a secret panel in the wall that still hung ajar— and had thus staged our fight in perhaps the most public place on campus. Dozens of students and faculty had just returned from the war game only to find us writhing about on the floor like a couple of idiots.

"He started it," Chip said, pointing at me.

"I did not!" I protested.

"I don't care who started it!" the principal roared. "Fighting isn't allowed at the academy!"

"But we fight all the time in class," Chip said.

"That's for a grade!" the principal snapped. "Unsanctioned fighting is different. I want to see you two in my office right now!"

The students all went "ooooh" in response. None of them wanted to be in our shoes.

I sat up, feeling ashamed and frightened, noting familiar faces in the crowd. Zoe seemed impressed I'd taken on Chip. Warren (who was still royal blue from head to toe) seemed annoyed Zoe was impressed. Murray looked concerned for me. Hauser and Stubbs looked concerned for Chip. Tina, my RA, appeared embarrassed, as though my behavior somehow reflected badly on her. Professor Crandall didn't seem to have any idea what was going on; he was too busy trying to dislodge some ice that had frozen in his eyebrows.

And then Erica emerged.

It was strange to see her in a crowd. Erica was such a loner, she seemed out of place surrounded by people.

Even stranger, she knelt by my side and cradled my face in her hands. "Are you okay?" she asked. It was such a gentle and caring gesture, I briefly wondered if someone had substituted the real Erica with a double agent. From the reaction of most of the other students, they were wondering the same thing. But it was definitely Erica: She had the same wonderful lilac and gunpowder smell as usual, along with a hint of latex paint.

"I've been better," I replied. Then I leaned in and whispered, "There's a bomb under the school."

Erica betrayed nothing. Her expression didn't change. I might as well have told her that I liked rabbits. I was wondering if she'd even heard me, but as she helped me to my feet, she whispered back, "I'm on it. I'll be in touch."

I didn't have time to ask anything else. The principal pointed upstairs toward his office. Chip and I dutifully followed him.

As we did, Chip whispered something to me as well. "Say one word about what you saw down there and you're dead."

The crowd parted for us, and I noticed the looks on my fellow students' faces had changed. They didn't seem to be pitying me for earning the principal's wrath anymore. Instead, they were looking at me curiously, wondering how on earth *I* had managed to earn Erica's concern. Many of the guys looked more impressed than they had upon learning I'd fended off an assassin.

Which made getting attacked by Chip and marched off to the principal's office almost seem worthwhile.

Almost. But not quite.

PROVOCATION

Principal's Office
February 8
1520 hours

The principal was five minutes into his tirade before I discovered what Erica had meant about being in touch.

I wasn't paying much attention to the tirade. I'm not sure the principal was either. He was talking to hear himself talk, railing on and on about how the academy held its students to a very high standard and how Chip and I had fallen very short of that and how if either one of us expected to graduate to a dignified field position with such behavior, then we were in for a rude awakening. In fact, we were lucky he didn't bounce us out of the school right then and there. . . .

I was surprised to find myself so calm in the face of the storm. In my previous 1,172 days of public school, I'd never gotten in trouble, let alone been sent to the principal's office. But, though I wasn't happy with the situation, I also knew the principal *couldn't* kick me out. His entire mole hunt was based on me being there. In fact, he could have frightened me more by threatening to keep me enrolled.

However, the *real* reason I wasn't very concerned by the principal was that I had plenty of other things to be very concerned about. Like what Chip and Hauser had been doing in the tunnel.

Had that really been a bomb down there? And what were they doing with it? Did it work? Were they trying to make it work? And if so, why?

What was Scorpio? It sounded like a code name for an operation, but what was the operation? Was the name "Scorpio" a key to explaining it? I knew Scorpio was a mythological giant scorpion—an extremely dangerous beast who had defeated Orion, the almost-invincible hunter. Scorpio was also a constellation and a sign of the zodiac for the duration of October 23 to November 22. Was that a clue? Was Scorpio scheduled to take place then? If so, it was a long way off.

I was glad I'd had a chance to tell Erica about the bomb. Hopefully, she was investigating it while we sat there. I even considered telling the principal about it, but I didn't want to do so right in front of Chip. Back in public school, if someone told you something like "Say one word about what you saw down there and you're dead," you could assume it was an exaggeration. At spy school, they actually taught you how to back those words up—and gave you the weapons to do it.

Erica was probably far more competent than the principal anyhow. She'd most likely already tracked down the bomb, dismantled it, and figured out who was behind it. Or so I hoped. I was desperate to get out of that office—not merely to find out what was going on, but also to evacuate the building just in case the bomb went off and reduced the place to toothpicks. (I briefly considered that the bomb probably wasn't live, because if it was, then Chip would have been sweating buckets. But then I also considered that, if Chip was as incompetent as Erica said, he wouldn't have any idea if the bomb was live or not—and thus, fearing for my life was still prudent.)

Unfortunately, the principal didn't show any signs of winding down. "Trying to hurt each other is unacceptable," he was saying. "You're supposed to try to hurt our *enemies*, for Pete's sake."

"Hello, Ben," Erica said.

I snapped upright in my seat, startled. Erica sounded as

though she were right behind me. I started to turn around. . . .

"Don't turn around!" Erica ordered.

So I didn't.

"Don't do *anything*," she continued. "And don't respond to me. I'm not in the room. You're the only one who can hear me."

I suddenly realized Erica's voice wasn't coming from behind me at all. Instead, it seemed to be coming from *inside* me. Like it was a thought in my head.

"I slipped a miniature Wi-Fi transmitter into your ear downstairs," Erica explained. "Which means I can hear everything that windbag's saying."

I frowned. So *that* was why Erica had cradled my face. It hadn't been affection at all. It was merely a ruse to wire me.

Having a transmitter in your ear is extremely unsettling. Your gut instinct when someone talks to you—or tells you they've slipped a piece of technology into your head without your permission—is to talk back. It took every ounce of control I had to not respond.

As it was, Chip was already eyeing me suspiciously. My startled response to Erica's first words had grabbed his attention. The principal was still lost in his own world, however. He was so caught up in his pontificating, he wouldn't have noticed a herd of elephants stampeding through the room.

"You're exactly where I need you to be," Erica told me.

"Now, I need you to do two things: First, I need you to pay attention to the principal. Not what he says. What he does. I don't want you to take your eyes off him for an instant. Try to remember everything. . . . Second, I need you to insult him."

What?! I wanted to ask. I *almost* did. It took an incredible amount of self-restraint not to. I couldn't imagine why Erica could possibly want me to get into even more trouble. But due to the one-sided nature of our communication, there was no way I could ask her.

"I know it's asking a lot, but you have to trust me." Erica's voice was soothing and confident. "I promise you, everything's going to work out fine."

For some reason, I believed her. Maybe because Erica was the only person I trusted. Maybe because her words inside my head made me think they were actually *my* words. Most likely, I just wanted to impress her. I probably would have stepped in front of a locomotive if she asked nicely enough. So I looked for an opportunity to cause trouble—and it wasn't long before I found it.

"When I was a student here, we *knew* how to behave," the principal chided. "Would you like to know how we were punished for fighting back then?"

"Wow, that would have been a *long* time ago," I said. "Did they put you in the stockade? They used that a lot in Colonial America."

The principal wheeled on me. "What did you just say?"

"That you're old," I replied. "Was I being too subtle for you?"

To my side, Chip's eyes had gone wide. I couldn't tell for sure, as I was keeping my gaze locked on the principal, but he might have been impressed by me.

Erica certainly was. "That's perfect!" she crowed. "Keep it up!"

The principal turned as red as the bottom of a baboon. He stormed toward me, getting right in my face. "Am I to assume, Mr. Ripley, that you think you're not already in enough trouble today? Are you asking for an even worse punishment?"

"Whatever it is, it couldn't be worse than your breath," I said. "What'd you have for lunch, dog poo?"

This time Chip snickered audibly.

The principal recoiled from me. For a few moments he seemed completely unsure what to do. Apparently, no student had ever talked to him like I'd just done. It looked like he wanted to expel me on the spot—only, he couldn't, and so he could only grow more apoplectic at the situation. His eyes bugged out from his face and he ran his fingers through his fake hair. "That's it!" he finally snapped. "I'm putting you on total probation!"

"Make him do it now," Erica told me.

"Fine," I said. "Let's do it."

Once again, the principal seemed thrown. All his threats seemed to be having the opposite effect he wanted. "Right now?"

"Right now," Erica said.

"Right now," I repeated.

"All right then, Buster. You got it." The principal went behind his desk, then stared at his computer blankly. After a few moments he snatched a dictionary off the shelf behind him, flipped it open—as though he needed help remembering how to spell his password—then snapped it shut and logged on. He then began to compose an e-mail, dictating what he was writing for my benefit. "To the attention of all academy staff: First-year student Benjamin Ripley is hereby placed on total probation until further notice from this office. . . ."

"Hey." The whisper was so soft, it took me a moment to realize it wasn't coming from Erica. It was Chip.

I flicked my eyes over to him.

"That was awesome," he said, one decibel above a whisper.

"Thanks," I whispered back.

". . . and will be denied all standard student privileges from this moment hence," the principal finished, then fixed me with a hard stare. "You mess with the bull—and you get the horns."

"That's funny," I replied. "When I look at you, I think of the *other* end of the bull."

"Whoa there, Tiger," Erica said. "You can take it easy now. Job's done."

It would have been nice if she'd told me that *before* I'd said anything else. My final insult had pushed the principal over the edge. So much anger surged through him, I expected lava to spew out of his ears. His lousy toupee had come unmoored from his head and was now askew, giving him the appearance of a poorly frosted cupcake. He stormed back to where I sat and jabbed a stubby finger at my nose. "All right, you little wisenheimer. You don't think I can get tougher? Then let's bring the hammer down. From now on, you're sleeping in the Box."

"But . . . I'm already sleeping in the Box," I said.

The principal's face went blank. "You are? Since when?"

"Uh . . . since I got here," I replied.

"Why?" he demanded. "What idiot put you in the Box?"

I winced, knowing he wasn't going to like the answer. "*You* did."

To my side, Chip was trying so hard not to laugh, *he* was turning red. The principal didn't notice, though. My last answer, true as it may have been, had revved up his ire. His entire body trembled with rage.

Before he could lash into me again, I tried to explain.

"An assassin tried to kill me in my room, remember? So you assigned me to stay in the Box for my safety."

The principal hesitated again, apparently caught between fury and confusion. "And you're still there?" he asked, in a furiously confused tone.

"No one ever told me I could move out," I answered.

"Well, you can't!" the principal snapped petulantly. "But not because it isn't safe. Because you're being punished for insubordination. And you're going to stay in the Box until I decide otherwise. You've crossed a line, mister. From now on, I am going to make it my personal mission to see that you are as miserable as possible for the rest of your time here!" He pressed a red button on his desk.

An instant later two armed agents burst into the room, guns drawn. They both looked surprised—and then disappointed—to see there were only two students sitting before the principal rather than, say, some enemy agents.

"Escort Mr. Ripley directly to the Box," the principal ordered.

"Uh . . . ," one of the agents said, "that red button is supposed to be used only for emergencies."

"This *is* an emergency!" the principal barked. "This boy's behavior has been downright mutinous. An example must be made." He swung his gaze back toward me. "Mark my words, Ripley. You will rue the day you ever met me."

"I already do." I couldn't help saying it, even though Erica hadn't asked me to. It didn't seem possible that anything I said could get me into *more* trouble.

The agents might not have been thrilled with the principal's order, but as he was a superior officer, they followed it, grabbing me by the arms, hoisting me to my feet, and marching me out of the office.

Chip Schacter walked right out behind us. The principal had grown so upset with me, he'd evidently forgotten that he'd originally called *both* of us in for a talking-to.

"Ripley, you might be a fraud and a liar, but you also have some serious guts," Chip said.

"Thanks," I replied.

Chip's stare grew menacing. "Though you'd still better keep your mouth shut about you-know-what."

The agents dragged me away before I could reply.

So I'd earned a tiny bit of Chip Schacter's respect—and possibly Erica's—and all I'd had to do was get myself in so much trouble with the principal that my remaining years at spy school were going to be nonstop misery.

It didn't exactly seem like the best trade-off in the world. I just prayed Erica knew what she was doing.

ANALYSIS

The Box

February 8

1600 hours

It wasn't until I had been perp-walked past the entire student body and locked in the Box for the night that it finally occurred to me to check my phone for messages. Things had been so hectic, I'd never read the text that had alerted Chip to my presence in the first place.

It was from Mike.

Another Pasternak party tomorrow night. Want me to spring you?

A month before, this would have been the greatest message I'd ever received. Now it was only another reminder of how lousy my life was at the academy. Mike was now a regular guest at Elizabeth Pasternak's, while I'd spent my afternoon being pummeled and manipulated—and was now under lockdown for the next five and a half years. Public school: 1. Spy school: -1,000.

Sure, Mike, I wanted to write back. *I'd love for you to spring me. FYI, you'll need a commando team and a getaway car.*

As it was, I couldn't even fire off a lame excuse about why I couldn't go. The Box had the Wi-Fi coverage of a coal mine. None.

I might have been less miserable if I'd heard from Erica, but there'd been radio silence ever since the principal's office. I still had no idea why Erica had made me bait the principal or, for that matter, if she had tracked down the bomb. If she hadn't, that meant I was now locked on a basement level with a live explosive device.

If it even was a live explosive device. I realized that I'd never gotten a very good look at it. . . .

Although I still could. I suddenly remembered I'd been taking a picture of the bomb right when I got the text from Mike. I quickly dug out Peachin's *Field Guide to Bombs and Other Incendiary Devices* and then brought up the photo on my phone.

Turned out, I'd taken a really fantastic picture . . . of the eyepiece of the digital scope. I had no photographic evidence of the bomb at all.

I sighed and flopped onto my bed, feeling depressed and useless. Not to mention imprisoned. Somewhere up on ground level, Zoe and my other newfound friends were probably celebrating their war game victory in a student lounge or practicing kill shots on the firing range. Meanwhile, I was totally isolated.

There was nothing I could do except homework. I cracked open Forsyth's *Basics of Cryptography*, read until my eyes went bleary, then looked at my clock and saw it was only four thirty in the afternoon.

Time really crawled when you were on lockdown.

I struggled through another chapter, nodding off seventeen or eighteen times, then checked my clock again.

It was still four thirty in the afternoon.

Either time *really* crawled when you were on lockdown or my clock was broken.

I checked my phone. In fact, it was eight thirty at night, which explained why I was so darn hungry. No one had come to get me for dinner. I wondered if this was part of my punishment or if the administration had simply forgotten about me. I'd now been at spy school long enough to guess it was the latter, which began to worry me. I could get through the night without food, but if someone didn't remember I was in the Box by the next morning, things could get dicey.

Still, it wasn't worth panicking yet. Maybe this was merely a test to see how I handled pressure. If so, I'd show them I was a tough egg to crack. For the benefit of any cameras that might have been on me, I played it cool, as though I were really enjoying being on lockdown. I laid back on my cot and gave a contented sigh. "This is great," I said to any concealed microphones. "All this time to myself. It's like being on vacation."

Then I casually examined my clock to see if I could keep it from telling me that it was eternally four thirty in the afternoon.

After a minute it occurred to me that I didn't have the slightest idea how to fix a clock. So I did the only thing I could think of. I pounded my fist on the top.

It worked. The clock started ticking again.

Just out of interest, I pounded on it once more. It stopped.

I pounded on it a third time. It started again. I cranked the time up to 8:31 p.m., then wondered exactly how to kill the next three hours until bedtime.

I dug out Dyson's *How to Stay Alive,* which wasn't exactly a cure for boredom. It was amazing how spy school textbooks could take any theoretically fascinating subject and make it as exciting as reading assembly instructions. I attempted to bone up on the basics of hand-to-hand combat, which should have been not only interesting, but also relevant to my current situation. I was asleep within minutes.

I woke to the disturbingly familiar sensation of someone pinioning my arms and slapping a hand over my mouth. It was too dark to see my attacker, but thankfully, she smelled like lilacs and gunpowder.

"Hi, Erica," I said, though my greeting was muffled by her hand.

"You might want to read the chapter on sleeping lightly, just in case someone who's actually dangerous breaks into your room next time." Although Erica's words were harsh, her tone wasn't quite as cold as usual, as though she might have actually been smiling as she said it. My staying calm under the circumstances had impressed her.

She took her hand off my mouth and sat on the bed.

"I assume you've dismantled the microphones?" I asked.

"Naturally," Erica replied.

My eyes flicked to my clock: 9:10 p.m.

"You're here earlier than I expected," I said.

"It's one a.m. sleepyhead. You really need to get a new clock."

The truth was, I *hadn't* expected her. I'd only been really hoping she'd show up. I was proud of myself for playing it so cool, though I hoped she couldn't hear my heart thumping in the dark. "Did you find the bomb?"

"No."

Now I tensed up, unable to control my fear. "You mean it's still out there . . . ?"

"Keep your panties on, Alice. I couldn't find it because it's not there anymore."

"You're sure you didn't miss it?"

If it was actually possible to do so, I heard Erica frown. "This is *me* we're talking about. I cased all subterranean levels of the campus. Even the ones I'm not supposed to know about. There's no bomb down here."

"This one was back in some pipes on the first level—"

"About twenty yards from a pallet full of powdered eggs. I know. I found where the bomb *was*. But like I said, it's gone. All that was left was a residue of C4 explosive putty. And a faint whiff of Chip Schacter's toxic aftershave. That's what you were fighting about? You saw him down there with it?"

"Yes. Him and Hauser. They came in through a secret entrance by the toolshed while—"

"I was capturing the flag. Yeah, I saw you going after him."

"Through a snowstorm while you were fighting a dozen guys?"

"I'm good at multitasking."

"Of course. Why didn't you follow us then?"

"Because I had to go get the mini-microphone so I could plant it on you once you got busted for fighting."

I thought about that for a second. "Don't you mean 'just in case' I got busted for fighting?"

"No," Erica replied. "I figured there was an exceptionally good chance Chip would spot you and then try to kick your ass."

I winced, embarrassed by my poor performance—and how predictable it was. "So . . . Chip removed the bomb after I caught him with it?"

"That's one possibility, though not one I favor."

"Why not?"

"Because Chip got a D-minus on his last bomb defusion final. If that moron had tried to do anything with a bomb, we'd know, because there'd be a huge smoking crater where the school used to be."

A thought came to me. "Then . . . that means he probably didn't plant the bomb either."

"You thought he did?" Erica asked in a disdainful tone.

"Uh . . . well . . . yes," I admitted. "He's kind of a jerk."

"Jerks hang you up from the flagpole by your underwear. They don't blow up schools."

"So then how'd he know about the bomb?"

"I don't know. Maybe he just stumbled across it."

"And he didn't tell anyone?"

"Well, as you saw, he told Hauser."

"But not anyone in the administration. That's suspicious, isn't it?"

"Yes."

"Why didn't he?"

Erica shrugged. "I'm still working on that. Though there's a few more pressing questions."

"Like: 'Who put the bomb down there if Chip didn't?'"

"Yes, like that."

"Do you think whoever put the bomb there is the one who also removed it?" I asked.

"It's possible. Once they realized Chip, Hauser, and you knew about it, they yanked it. But there's some questions about that as well."

"Like what?"

"Like where the bomb was in the first place. If I were a bomber looking to cause some serious trouble here, I'd have set the bomb under one of the main buildings. But this one was out under the woods, next to a storage room for the mess hall. If it had gone off, all it would have done was blow up a couple trees and a lot of canned peas."

"Maybe the bomber was only looking to cause a little bit of trouble," I suggested. "To send a message or something."

"What message does blowing up a bunch of canned peas send?" Erica asked.

"Um . . . stop serving us canned peas?"

"I think you could probably get that point across with an e-mail."

"Not if you wanted to ensure there were no more canned peas to serve."

"Drop the canned peas thing, Ben. It's not going to fly."

I backed down, then thought of something else. "Are there security cameras in the tunnels?"

"No."

"Really? But there's cameras everywhere aboveground."

"Yes," Erica said. "I think the idea was, if you've got enough cameras aboveground, you shouldn't need any below. After all, the only people who are supposed to even *know* there's a subterranean level here are the students and faculty, who are all theoretically good guys."

"But if one of them decides to work for the enemy . . ."

"It's not such a good idea anymore. Good point. Of course, it's also possible that there's no cameras down here because they're expensive and there's about thirteen miles of tunnels they'd have to wire. Whatever the reason, there's no cameras. Thus no footage of anyone setting or removing the bomb."

"Should *we* tell the administration?"

"What? That there *used* to be a bomb down here, but now it's gone? They'll never believe that."

"You said there was residue."

"Yes. There. *was*. I took it." Erica held up an evidence bag. There was a trace amount of yellow putty in it.

I eyed it cautiously, aware that even that tiny bit of explosive was enough to vaporize us. "So what do we do now?"

"Isn't it obvious?" Erica asked. "It's time to hack the mainframe."

INFILTRATION

Principal's Office
February 9
0300 hours

There was only one place in the entire thirteen
miles of subterranean tunnels beneath the campus that actually had security cameras: the hallway directly outside the Box. Just in case any prisoners—or students—being held there tried to escape.

However, Erica had already taken care of them. It was relatively simple to do. She simply jacked into each camera from behind and froze the image it transmitted. A still frame of an empty hallway looked exactly like live footage of an empty hallway.

"It's precisely what the assassin did to all the cameras when he paid you a visit," she explained.

"It doesn't look very difficult to take the cameras out of commission," I said.

"No, it's not. But you *do* have to know where they all are. Which your standard bad guy infiltrating the school wouldn't—unless someone inside the school had told him."

Erica knew the location of every camera on campus. All 1,672 of them. We had to jack sixty-three to get through the Hale Building and up to the principal's office, as well as doing a bit of zigzagging and shimmying to avoid fifty-eight others. Even moving at a good clip, it still took us well over an hour to get there, during which time Erica forced me to be absolutely silent.

The computerized keypad by the principal's office door that I'd fried with the Taser during my SACSAs had been replaced by a shiny new one, but Erica already knew the entry code.

It was 12345678.

"The principal isn't very good at remembering codes," she explained once we were inside, after jacking both cameras in his office. "He's also an idiot."

"So wouldn't the code to access the mainframe be the same?" I suggested.

"Sadly, no. Though I *did* try it. The CIA itself runs the

mainframe, not the school. And they're a little more protective of it than the principal is of his office. As you know, there's a sixteen-bit daisy-chain encryption on it."

"Yes. But I still have no idea what that means."

Erica sighed. "Haven't you read *Basics of Cryptography* yet?"

"I keep trying to. But that book is mind-numbing. Reading it is like inhaling chloroform."

"Spoken like someone who's never inhaled chloroform," Erica groused. "A sixteen-bit daisy chain is a sixteen-character entry code that is randomly selected by the CIA mainframe every day. It's impossible to crack. The code is e-mailed to everyone's secure account the day before, so the only way you can know the code is to have access to the mainframe in the first place. Then, in theory, you're supposed to commit each day's code to memory."

"But the principal doesn't," I concluded.

Erica rewarded me with one of her rare smiles. "Exactly. Remembering it requires too much brainpower."

"You know that for a fact?"

"It's more of an extremely well-informed assumption. The principal is lucky he can remember which foot to put forward when he walks across a room. Now, this is where *you* come in. Think back to this afternoon. What did the principal do before he logged on to the mainframe?"

Understanding suddenly dawned on me. "That's why you had me insult him? To get him to log on and e-mail everyone?"

"Exactly."

"Wasn't there a way to do that that didn't involve him getting furious at me?"

"Possibly. But this way worked. So tell me: What happened in here?"

I did my best to reconstruct the events of the afternoon. "He threatened me with probation."

"And then . . . ?"

"You told me to make him go through with it. So I did. Then he went to the computer, but he blanked at first."

"Because he couldn't remember his log-in code. Perfect." Erica approached me, her eyes alive with excitement. "What did he do next?"

Now *I* blanked. Her eyes were dazzling and her breath smelled like cinnamon Trident. I didn't want to disappoint her, so, of course, my brain shut down completely. I strained to remember what had happened, but it seemed that the harder I tried, the blurrier everything got.

"I'm sorry," I apologized. "I can't remember."

Erica came even closer, until she was only a few inches away, looking right into my eyes. "If you tell me, I'll give you a hug."

"He opened the dictionary," I said immediately. It was automatic. Some part of my reptile brain had triggered, desperate for contact from her.

Erica smiled, pleased with herself. "That's my boy." Then, instead of giving me my reward, she went to the bookshelf and grabbed the dictionary.

"Um . . . ," I said. "Didn't you say you would give me a hug?"

"Yes. But I didn't say when."

"Oh. I kind of assumed it'd be *now*."

"Which was a mistake. Not very good negotiating on your part." Erica flipped the dictionary open on the desk and found what she was looking for right inside the front cover. "Ah! Here we go!"

A three-by-five-inch index card was taped there. Thirty-two previous sixteen-character entry codes had already been written on it and crossed out. The card was almost full. When it was, the principal would probably shred it and then tape a new card into the cover; there were plenty of Scotch tape remnants indicating this card was one of hundreds that had been taped there over the years.

The last entry code was h\$Kp8*&cc:Qw@m?x.

Erica booted up the principal's computer, brought up the log-in page for the mainframe, and entered the code.

Mainframe access granted, the computer told us.

"We're in!" Erica crowed.

She was smiling broadly now, in her element. She seemed to forget about me as her fingers danced across the keyboard. Giving her access to the CIA's secret files was like giving a normal kid the keys to Disneyland. Every once in a while, she would pause momentarily, say "Wow" or "That's interesting," and then go right back to searching the files again.

I tried to watch what she was doing over her shoulder, but the pages flew past too quickly, one every few seconds. Maybe she was speed-reading them; maybe she was only scanning the first sentences and moving on. There was never time to ask.

Finally, Erica gave a triumphant laugh. She'd found what she was looking for. "Here we go, Ben. Everyone who received a hard copy of your personal file. See if anyone there rings a bell."

She printed out the page and handed it to me. There were thirteen names on it.

The first was the director of the CIA.

The next five were names I didn't recognize: Percy Thigpen, Eustace McCrae, Robert Friggoletto, Eleanor Haskett, Xavier Gonzalez. "Who are these people?" I asked.

"High-ranking muckety-mucks at the CIA. The folks who approved your recruitment." Erica was already back on the computer again, now typing something. "They all keep a pretty low profile. I didn't expect you to know them. But still, couldn't hurt to ask."

The next name on the list was Alexander Hale.

The one after that made me laugh.

"Who on earth is Barnabus Sidebottom?" I asked.

"You're in his office right now," Erica replied.

"The principal's name is Barnabus Sidebottom?"

"Yes."

"I can see why he prefers to keep that a secret," I said.

I thought I heard Erica laugh, though when I looked over at her, she was wiping her nose. Or at least pretending to wipe her nose so that I wouldn't *think* I'd made her laugh.

I returned my attention to the list. The next four names were professors at spy school. I knew a bit about all of them; Murray, Zoe, and Warren had given me the lowdown on the entire faculty so I'd know whose classes to take and whose to avoid like the plague.

Joseph Crouch was a professor of cryptology, the only one of the four I'd had a class with so far; he'd substituted one day when my regular cryptography teacher had the flu. (At least, the school *claimed* he had the flu. Zoe suspected he'd actually been called away on a top secret mission.) Crouch was an old-timer, though he'd kept his wits about him and could deliver a riveting lecture. However, he was also so smart that he could be tremendously difficult to follow.

"Is Crouch the one who developed my 'cryptography skills' for me?" I asked.

"I'd assume so." Erica was so engrossed in whatever she was typing on the computer, she didn't even look up.

Kieran Murphy taught the intricacies of going undercover for years at a time. His was an extremely advanced class, reserved for only sixth-year students, with the extremely rare and talented fifth year making the cut. Professor Murphy was one of the finest undercover agents the CIA had ever had, having served several multiyear tours of duty that were completely classified, though there was a rumor that he'd done so well passing himself off as a loyal agent in a terrorist cell that the cell's leader had asked him to serve as best man at his wedding.

Harlan Kelly taught disguise. I thought I'd seen him only once or twice, though I wasn't sure. No one really knew how many times they'd seen Harlan, as he had a habit of showing up on campus as a completely different person every day. And not always a male person. Murray claimed the principal had once hit on a visiting female professor for half an hour before discovering she was actually Harlan.

Lydia Greenwald-Smith taught counterespionage. She was a good instructor, but that was all anyone knew about her. She was all business in class and kept her life outside of school as private as possible. According to my friends, there were slime molds with more personality.

The final name on the list was the only one that really surprised me.

Tina Cuevo.

"Tina's on here," I said.

"Yeah, I saw that." Erica still didn't look up from her typing. Her fingers were flying furiously across the keyboard, as though a manifesto were pouring out of her.

"Does that seem strange to you?" I asked.

"Why?"

"She's the only student."

"Yes, but she was also supposed to be your resident adviser, until you got put in the Box. Since you were a potential target for enemy operatives, it probably made sense to notify her so she could monitor your safety."

I thought back to the first time I encountered Tina, the night the assassin had come to my room. She'd had a gun in the pocket of her pajamas. And she'd reacted very quickly to my claim that there was an assassin down the hall. She hadn't even questioned it, but had immediately gone off to deal with the situation. In retrospect, that all made more sense if she already knew I was mole bait. And yet . . .

"She still might be worth investigating," I said. "Chip was one of the first people to know about my crypto skills."

"No, he was one of the first people to *admit* that he knew about your crypto skills."

"Even so, he's a student. What seems more likely—that he got that information from Tina or from one of his professors?"

"I can't imagine Tina ever sharing classified information with Chip," Erica said. "She's ranked third in her class. They don't let just *anyone* be a resident adviser."

"Well, maybe Chip broke into her room, then."

"Tina's not dumb enough to leave a classified file out in the open where a yahoo like Chip could find it."

"Well, *someone* had to. And I doubt it was the head of the CIA."

Erica glanced up from the computer. "Just because a person has risen to a position of prominence doesn't mean they don't screw up now and then. I'd say any one of those professors could have just as easily leaked your info as Tina. With the possible exception of Kieran Murphy. You don't last very long as an undercover agent if you're prone to mistakes."

"But he did spend the most time among the enemy out of anyone. Maybe someone turned him along the way."

Erica frowned at the thought of this, but she didn't deny it was possible either. "We can always come back to the names on that list. But if phase two of our plan works out, we won't even need to investigate them. The enemy's going to come right to us."

Erica finished typing with a flourish, then pressed the enter button. The computer whirred into action.

I suddenly grew very worried. "Um . . . what's phase two?"

"The e-mail I just sent. Though I used the principal's e-mail account, so everyone will think *he* sent it."

"To whom?"

"A very select group of recipients, including but not limited to the twelve other people on your list."

All the warmth I'd ever felt toward Erica began to evaporate. "Erica? What have you done?"

"Me?" she asked coyly. "I haven't done anything. *You* have. In fact, you've just developed something even more important than Pinwheel. Congratulations."

"That's not funny."

Erica erased her search history and logged out of the mainframe. "Pinwheel was merely supposed to be an advancement in encrypting messages," she explained. "Pretty cool and all, but now the administration has learned you have something even bigger up your sleeve: Jackhammer. The ultimate code breaker. Able to demolish *any* encryption. A total game changer. The administration has arranged for you to give a highly classified presentation of it to them tomorrow night. Until then, they've put you on lockdown to protect you."

I winced, seeing where this was going. "Because if word

of this leaks out, anyone who wants Jackhammer is going to come after me."

"Exactly." Erica flicked off the computer and began to clean up any evidence that we'd been in the room. She was maddeningly nonchalant for someone who'd just deliberately put my life in jeopardy.

"You turned me into bait!" I exclaimed.

"You were *already* bait," Erica informed me.

"Well, *bigger* bait, then," I said. "Like shark chum. You know this is going to be leaked again."

"Of course it will. The mole won't be able to resist. But don't freak out. I also requested a complete security upgrade for you from CIA headquarters. They'll come through."

"If the enemy doesn't find some way to catch everyone with their pants down again!"

Erica took a packet of antiseptic wipes from her pocket and began to clean her fingerprints off the principal's desk. "Look, we can play this game one of two ways. You can sit around, waiting for the bad guys to come after you whenever they feel like it, or you can make them come to you on your own schedule. I chose option two. This way, we're prepared for them."

I steamed over that for a minute. As much as I hated to admit it, there was a good amount of logic to Erica's argument. But I was still annoyed. "You could have at least *told* me you were going to do this."

"I just did."

"I meant *before* you did it."

"If it's any consolation, I also cancelled your probation," Erica said. "As far as anyone knows, that order is directly from the principal. And as far as the principal knows, well . . . he's probably forgotten he ever put you on probation in the first place. If you want, you're free to move out of the Box and back into a real dorm room."

My anger at Erica began to dissipate, though I wasn't ready to be enamored of her again. She was using me just as much as the administration was, putting me in danger to advance her own agenda. "It'd probably be best to stay there one more night," I said. "At least until the CIA shows up tomorrow."

"I think that'd be wise." Erica cased the principal's office, decided it looked exactly as it had when we'd entered, then ushered me toward the door.

"What if the enemy suspects this is a ruse?" I asked.

"They probably will. But even then, they won't be able to fully discount it."

"Which means they're coming after me no matter what."

"Yes, it does." Erica flashed the biggest smile I'd ever seen her give. "Exciting, isn't it?"

EVIDENCE

The Mess
February 9
1310 hours

"I have one word of advice for you," Murray told me the next day at lunch. "Run."

"Run?" I repeated. "Run where?"

"Anywhere. Back home. The Lincoln Memorial. Las Vegas. I don't care. As long as you get away from here. Because if you stay here, you're going to die." Murray dug into a stack of peanut butter and jelly sandwiches he'd made himself. That wasn't a bad idea, given that the mess was serving sloppy joes that day.

"He can't run," Zoe countered. "That'll put him in *more*

danger. Check out all the security." She waved around the mess.

"Yeah," Warren chimed in. "This place is locked down tighter than Fort Knox."

There were, in fact, a dozen CIA agents in the room, all there to protect me. Some were actively stationed at the doors to the room, on alert, while others were more covert, pretending to be visiting faculty. Everyone knew they were really there to guard me, however; the academy would never have allowed visiting faculty to eat lunch in the mess for fear of poisoning them.

Erica's ploy had worked amazingly well. Everyone at the CIA she'd e-mailed about Jackhammer had bought it hook, line, and sinker, which was a little disturbing given that many of them were the top spies in the country. They'd believed the message had actually been sent by the principal—after all, his account was on the mainframe and the mainframe was supposed to be impenetrable. Thus, they'd also believed Jack-hammer existed and had to be protected at all costs. Security was arranged immediately. I'd been awakened at six a.m. that morning by a knock on my cell door. It was Alexander Hale, who'd been called in from another assignment (classified, of course) to oversee the operation. He'd come in so fast, he was still wearing a dashiki.

Unfortunately, the story had spread even faster than

Erica had predicted. The Academy's information security was leakier than the *Titanic*. I hadn't told my friends anything about Jackhammer, but they'd found out anyhow. The entire school had. Everyone knew everything before breakfast: that I'd invented the ultimate code breaker, that I was presenting it to the academy administration that evening . . . and that I was a marked man.

Alexander wasn't currently in the mess himself. He was out checking on his troops, who were posted all along the perimeter of the property, as at well as at various points of tactical significance on campus. In all, he'd informed me, there were fifty-two CIA agents on duty that day, all charged exclusively with keeping me safe.

There was also Erica. She'd faded into the background, but she hadn't let me out of her sight all day. (Even when I'd had to use the bathroom, which was a bit uncomfortable.) At the moment she was two tables away, theoretically reading Driscoll's *User's Guide to Southeast Asian Artillery* while eating a salad, but I knew she was even more finely tuned in to the goings on of the room than usual. Erica hadn't set up Jackhammer just to let the CIA swoop in and steal her thunder; when the heat came down, she intended to be in the thick of it.

She and I had spent the morning attempting to track down the source of the leak, but to no avail. The mole had covered their tracks well. Our investigation was an endless loop, everyone pointing the finger at someone else until we were right back where we'd started.

"Zoe's right," I said. "If I ditch this place, I'm a sitting duck."

"And if you stay here, you're a dead one." Murray had a wad of sandwich crammed into his cheek so large, he looked like a chipmunk hoarding nuts. "Consider this: What happens *after* you make your little presentation tonight? Once you spill the beans on Jackhammer, you're even more of a target. For good. You think the CIA's gonna pony up this much security every day for the rest of your life?"

I swallowed a bite of sloppy joe, concerned. I *hadn't* considered that. "But how does running away solve anything?" I asked. "Our enemies are still going to want Jackhammer whether I spill the beans or not."

"Well, you don't *just* run," Murray explained. "You have to start a disinformation campaign first. Spread the word that you never invented Jackhammer. It was all a ruse to flush out our enemies. In fact, you're not even Crypto Whiz Boy. You're merely a patsy brought in by the CIA as bait."

"Oh, yeah," Zoe scoffed. "Like anyone would ever believe that."

"Yeah," Warren agreed, as he did with virtually everything Zoe said. "That's ridiculous."

It was the perfect indication of how complicated my life had become: that telling the truth about myself would now be considered a disinformation campaign. And that no one would buy it anyhow.

"The genie's out of the bottle," I said. "There's no way to get it back in. The only way for me to be safe is for the CIA to nab whoever's after me."

"Ben's right," Zoe told Murray.

"Zoe's right about Ben being right," Warren agreed.

"Not necessarily." Murray turned to me. "Suppose someone tries to take you out today, and the agency nails him. That's not the guy running the operation. It's just some poor schmo who got stuck with a lousy assignment. Or, heck, maybe he's a freelance assassin who doesn't even *know* who hired him. Yes, that's a lead, but it could take the CIA years to figure out whom it leads *to*. And that's only one enemy organization. I'll bet there's a dozen who'd like to get their hands on Jackhammer. You think they're *all* going to strike today? You think the CIA's ever going to bring them *all* down?"

I swallowed again. I hadn't considered that, either. I glanced over at Erica, who was still riveted to her book. Had she thought of any of this? I wondered. It seemed unlikely she hadn't. Erica thought of everything, which meant she'd knowingly placed me in great danger for her own gain.

Even Zoe looked concerned, though she tried to put

some positive spin on it. She gave me a pat on the knee that was supposed to be reassuring and said, "Smokescreen can handle it. Remember, he's not just a brainiac. He's a lean, mean fighting machine."

"Well . . . he *did* abandon me in the heat of battle yesterday," Warren countered.

Zoe frowned at him. "First of all, you totally screwed up your synchronization and attacked too early. Second, he was on a mission, tailing Chip. And finally, he *didn't* abandon you. He only took off once he knew that Ice Queen had things under control."

Warren pouted sullenly in response, though I had to admit, I'd have been upset if I'd been in his position too. He'd been pelted with so many paintballs that, despite an hour in the shower, his skin was still light blue.

"I don't care how good Ben is," Murray said. "Even Alexander Hale couldn't handle everything that's gonna come at him." He crammed another half sandwich into his mouth.

"What's with all the peanut butter, Washout?" Zoe asked. "Your cholesterol's gonna go through the roof."

"I hope so," Murray replied. "I've got a physical to assess my readiness for the field next week. Speaking of which, I'm gonna go get pie. Who wants pie?"

"I'll take some," I said. "À la mode." If people were going to try to kill me that day, at the very least, I felt I deserved dessert.

"You got it." Murray hustled off to the lunch line.

Warren suddenly stiffened, looking behind me. "Oh. *That's* why Murray split in such a hurry."

I spun around and saw Chip Schacter, Greg Hauser, and Kirsten Stubbs making a beeline for me.

Virtually the entire mess hall went on alert. A hundred heads swiveled toward me. Everyone tensed, ready for another fight.

I felt unusually calm confronting Chip, however. Probably because there were twelve highly trained CIA agents close by, tasked with protecting my safety. If Chip so much as poked me too hard, he'd have been pummeled into pudding.

Chip took Warren's chair—even though Warren was sitting in it. He simply tilted it forward, dumping Warren to the floor, and then sat down facing me.

"I thought you were on ultra-super probation," he said. "What are you doing out here?"

I shrugged. "The principal changed his mind."

"Why?" Chip asked. "Because of this Jackrabbit thing?"

"Jackhammer," I corrected, wondering if there was *any-one* who didn't know about it, given that it was supposed to be top secret. "Maybe. I'm not really sure why the principal does anything."

"He's not the only one who's tough to figure out," Chip said. "The way you were busting his chops yesterday, it almost seemed like you *wanted* probation. And now today, it's like nothing ever happened."

"You busted the principal's chops?" Zoe asked me, her eyes growing bigger than usual.

"He didn't tell you?" Chip asked. "Ripley here had the principal so worked up, I thought the guy was gonna have an angerism."

"Aneurysm," I corrected.

Zoe gaped at me. "Are you psycho? Why would you do that?"

"Exactly my question," Chip said, giving me a hard stare. "Why would you?"

I tried to casually shrug it off. "The guy was just asking for it. Haven't you ever wanted to tell him what you actually thought of him?"

"Sure," Zoe said. "But not so badly that I'd risk getting bounced out of school for it."

"Well, maybe that's the thing," Chip said. "Maybe Ripley here *knows* he can't get bounced out of school."

The statement hung there for a moment. Zoe and Warren stared at me, partly wondering if this was true and partly stunned that Chip, of all people, had been the one to figure it out.

"Is this true?" Warren asked me. There was now a bit of suspicion in his eyes.

"Yeah, Ripley. What's the deal?" Chip echoed, although there was a strange, mocking lilt to his voice, as though he already knew the answer.

"I might, uh, have some immunity because of Jackhammer," I lied.

"Of course!" Zoe said. "You're not just a coding genius. You're *the* coding genius! They can't boot you, no matter what!"

"Maybe. Or maybe not," Chip said knowingly. He stood up, slapped a hand on my shoulder, then whispered in my ear. "I'm onto you, Ripley. Just thought you should know."

Then he and his goons headed to the lunch line. Chip didn't look back, though I noticed Hauser kept his eyes on me the whole time.

I realized my hands were shaking. The exchange with Chip had left me unsettled, my mind full of questions. How much did Chip actually know about me? Did he know the whole truth—and if so, did that make him the mole? Or had he found out some other way? Or did he only *think* he knew the truth, in which case, he wasn't the mole at all, but simply the knucklehead we had suspected all along? And what did all this have to do with the bomb under the school?

"What was that all about?" Murray sat back down beside me and slid over a large slice of banana pie à la mode. I guessed he'd been waiting for Chip to take off before coming back. For himself, he had two slices of pie and three scoops of ice cream topped by a mountain of whipped cream, all the better to boost his cholesterol.

"Just my daily dose of Chip Schacter intimidation," I said.

"Not quite," Zoe countered. "This was different. Chip seemed . . . Well, it's weird but . . . it kind of seemed like he *likes* you now."

"Really?" Murray's eyebrows arched so high, they disappeared into his hair. "What'd you do, pull a thorn out of his paw?"

"He mouthed off to the principal yesterday," Zoe said.

Murray's eyebrows went even higher. "You did? I'm trying to be the worst spy on campus, and even *I* won't do that. Are you psycho?"

"That's what I said," Zoe told him.

"Maybe he *is* psycho," Warren whispered, thinking it was too low for me to hear.

I didn't respond to it, though. Something else had grabbed my attention. There was something in the pocket of my jacket that hadn't been there a few minutes before. I wasn't sure *how* I knew exactly, as the jacket was slung over the back of my chair. I just had a sense that something was different, like there was the tiniest shift of weight. Maybe my spy senses were starting to kick in, I thought, giving me an extra awareness of everything going on around me.

Without trying to draw attention, I slipped my hand into the pocket. Sure enough, there was a folded piece of paper under my phone.

"Chip realized that the principal *can't* get rid of Ben," Zoe was saying. "Now that he's come up with Jackhammer, he's too important."

"Holy cow, Chip's right." Murray was impressed. "I hadn't thought of that. Ben, you're invincible! You need to take advantage of this! If you can't get kicked out, you don't have to do your homework. You don't even have to show up for class! You could fill the principal's car with shaving cream and he wouldn't be able to do a thing about it!"

"Yes, he could," Zoe shot back. "Just because the administration can't boot Ben doesn't mean they can't punish him."

"Yeah," Warren agreed.

While they were distracted, I shifted the piece of paper under the table and unfolded it.

Meet me in the library tonight. Midnight. Your life depends on it.

It wasn't signed, but I was pretty sure it was from Chip. For one thing, it looked like an ape had written it, and "library" had been misspelled. Also, I was almost positive the paper hadn't been in my pocket before I'd sat down to lunch—and Chip had just had the perfect opportunity to slip something to me when he'd whispered in my ear.

Now a whole new set of questions cropped up. What could Chip possibly have to talk to me about that my life depended on? If he was the mole, why approach me like this? If he wasn't, what did he know? Now that I thought about it, the note could be interpreted two ways: Either I had to meet up with Chip to discuss something that my life depended on . . . or he was threatening to end my life if I didn't meet up with him.

If it was even Chip who'd written the note. I realized that both Hauser and Stubbs had also had the chance to slip something into my pocket; they'd both been looming behind me while I was talking to Chip. Both of them seemed capable of misspelling "library." Maybe one of them wanted to talk to me without Chip knowing. Or maybe one of them wanted to lure me into a trap in the library.

Or maybe I was wrong and the note had been placed in my pocket *before* lunch. If so, practically anyone in the school could have slipped it to me.

Why couldn't they have just signed the darn note? I wondered. *Would it kill anyone at this school to be a little less cryptic for once?*

Unfortunately, I knew the answer to that question was probably yes.

I realized there was still a conversation going on at the

table. I'd filtered it out while thinking about the note, but now it floated back through my consciousness. Murray, Zoe, and Warren were now talking about Chip.

"No way he likes Ben," Murray was saying. "Even if it *looked* like he likes Ben, with Chip, there's always an ulterior motive."

"You weren't here," Zoe said. "You were hiding over in the dessert line until you knew it was safe to come back. I was right here, and I'm telling you, Chip was different. It actually seemed like he was trying to be nice."

"He didn't seem that nice to *me*," Warren responded.

"Well, that's because he hasn't had much practice," Zoe replied. "I think he was really trying to reach out to Smokescreen here. In a weird way, it was kind of sweet."

"Oh no," Warren gasped. "You *like* him, don't you?"

Zoe recoiled, offended. "What?"

"You *like* him," Warren said bitterly. "Just like all the other girls. You know he's a jerk, but since he's handsome, you keep hoping that deep down inside, he's really a nice guy."

"And deep down inside, you're an idiot," Zoe shot back. "I do not like Chip."

"Well if you do, forget about it," Murray said. "He and Tina are together."

I sat up, unable to control my surprise—although neither

could Zoe and Warren. "They are?" we all asked at once.

"You didn't know?" Murray replied. "What kind of spies are you?"

"Better than you," Zoe snapped. "How'd *you* know?"

"I notice things." Murray stuffed half a scoop of ice cream in his mouth. "They're trying to keep it a secret, obviously, but I've seen them getting some face time now and then."

My mind was racing now. If Chip and Tina were an item—and Tina was the one student given a hard copy of my file—then it would have been relatively easy for Chip to get his hands on it. Which would explain how he was the first one to show up at my door, knowing about my secret cryptographic abilities before *I* even knew about them. Erica had also kept Tina in the loop about Jackhammer, which explained why Chip had claimed to be onto me. And now he'd slipped a note into my pocket wanting me to meet him secretly. . . .

I had to tell Erica. I couldn't believe *she* didn't know about Tina and Chip—although, when I thought about it, if there was one thing the Ice Queen wasn't particularly well tuned to, it was interpersonal relationships.

"I have to go," I said, standing up from the table.

"Right now?" Murray asked. "You haven't even touched your pie!"

"I'm not hungry anymore," I said.

"Can I have it, then?" Murray asked.

"Sure." I grabbed my jacket and started across the room toward Erica.

She seemed to sense me coming before I'd taken three steps. She looked toward me, on guard, and I wondered if I was breaking some sort of protocol by approaching her in public.

But then I realized it wasn't only *me* she was looking at. She was taking in the whole room around me as well.

The CIA agents posted around the mess had all gone on alert. The two closest to me were rushing my way. One cut me off before I could get to Erica. The second swept in behind me, grasping my arm tightly and wheeling me toward the door.

"You need to come with us," she said. "Right now."

"Why?" I tried to hide the worry in my voice.

Alexander Hale burst into the mess ahead of us. A murmur of excitement rippled through the room, as though a movie star had entered. Alexander didn't seem to notice. Instead, he seemed relieved to see I was all right.

"Your Jackhammer presentation has been cancelled," he informed me. "We've just received some intel from the field. We have to get you somewhere safe right now."

"Safer than a campus surrounded by CIA agents?" I asked.

"Yes," Alexander replied. "The enemy's coming for you."

SECURITY

Security Room
February 9
1330 hours

Alexander Hale took me directly to the security room, the command center of the entire academy.

It was a large bunker tucked away in the labyrinth of tunnels under the campus. Alexander insisted it was the most secure location for twenty miles in any direction, although I figured that was probably an exaggeration, since the White House and the Pentagon were both less than ten miles away.

It *did* look impressive from the outside, however. Two CIA agents bristling with weapons flanked a thick steel door with a high-tech entry system.

Alexander typed a code on a keypad, had his palm and retina scanned, then said "My dog has fleas" into a microphone that analyzed his voice.

"Entry approved," a lush feminine voice replied.

The door didn't budge, though.

Alexander pounded on it, annoyed. "Open up in there!" he yelled. "The stupid security door's on the fritz again!"

There was a click, and an embarrassed-looking agent opened the door from the inside.

"Lousy high-tech entry systems," Alexander muttered under his breath. "This is what happens when the government subcontracts everything to the lowest bidder." Then he caught himself and smiled at me reassuringly. "It's still secure, though! If it's that much trouble for *me* to get in, imagine how difficult it'd be for the enemy."

Although it hadn't been an auspicious beginning, I had to admit the room *felt* safe. I could now see that the door was nearly a foot thick with a dead bolt as big as a tyrannosaurus femur. The room was surrounded by imposing cement walls plated with steel. When the door slammed shut again, it felt as though we were encased in an iron womb.

Along one wall was a panel of twelve video monitors linked to the campus security camera system. Two CIA agents sat at computer terminals before the panel, which allowed them to bring up the live feed from any camera they wished.

Two more agents—one of whom had just opened the door for us—flanked the entrance from the inside. Within the room itself were two more computer terminals and a passage to another area.

"What's down that way?" I asked Alexander.

"Living quarters," he replied. "In case anyone needs to stay down here for the long haul. Have a peek if you'd like."

The passage led to a spare living space. There were eight cots and dressers, two showers, some imitation-leather couches arranged around a squat coffee table, a small kitchenette and—because this bunker dated back to the Cold War—a full bar. Alexander went to the refrigerator and got himself a neon yellow sports drink. It looked like a radioactive urine sample.

"How long do people usually stay down here?" I asked.

Alexander shrugged. "Not very long. This was all built quite some time ago, when the higher-ups expected the Russians might take over the country at any instant. I won't kid you, there've been a few scares over the years, but never anything serious. All troubles were attended to with great dispatch. I think the longest anyone ever had to be sequestered down here was a week."

"Have you ever had a situation like *this* before?" I asked.

Alexander hesitated for a half second too long before answering, then realized he'd done it and owned it. "Not exactly. But don't worry. We have the best of the best out there, working to protect you. And I'm in charge. I once had to protect the queen of Saudi Arabia from a horde of terrorists with nothing but a Swiss Army knife, and she made it through without a scratch. You're going to be fine. Energy drink?" Alexander waved to the refrigerator.

I shook my head. My stomach was too jittery to handle anything. My lunch was already threatening to make a return trip—although this was routine for sloppy joe days. "When you said the enemy is coming for me, what did that mean, exactly? Do they want to capture me . . . or kill me?"

"I'll be honest with you: We're not sure." Alexander sat on one couch and waved me to the other. "If I were a betting man, I'd say they're looking to extract you. Someone with your talents is worth far more alive than dead. But I can't guarantee that. You need to be on your guard at all times. Do you have a weapon on you?"

"Uh, no," I admitted. It was recommended that students at spy school carry weapons at all times, even when they didn't have an active threat against their lives—and many did. But even though I'd been putting in a lot of time on the shooting range lately, I'd somehow managed to get *less* accurate. The head instructor, Justin "Deadeye" Pratchett, had even suggested it was safer for me to *not* have a loaded weapon—although he had given me a realistic-looking toy gun so I could bluff my way out of trouble without shooting myself in the foot. I told Alexander this and showed him the dummy gun.

Alexander tutted disapprovingly. "If the going gets rough—not that it's going to, of course—you're going to need more than a toy." He thumped the coffee table, and a secret panel slid open, revealing a dozen guns crammed inside, ranging from pistols to assault rifles. "And just in case," Alexander said, "there's a portable missile launcher in a panel behind the bar."

I eyed the guns warily, then glanced back down the hall toward the command center. Everything had been quiet since we'd arrived. Either the agents monitoring the security cameras hadn't seen anything that concerned them, or they *had* seen something and done an incredible job of keeping calm about it. "What was the intel you got about the enemy?"

"We picked up some chatter. The Agency has several massive computers devoted solely to monitoring every bit of electronic communication," Alexander said. "Land lines, cell phones, satellite links, e-mail, Twitter feeds . . ."

"We actually think the terrorists are going to Tweet their plans?" I asked.

"We don't want to rule out anything," Alexander cautioned. "I once was able to bring down an entire terrorist cell in Kandahar because one of them posted pictures of their hideout on his Facebook page. Anyhow, we plugged the word 'Jackhammer' into the matrix this morning and got a hit right before I came to get you."

I perched on the edge of the sofa, worried. "What'd it say?"

"The system doesn't quite work like that," Alexander explained. "It has to sort through an unfathomable amount of information. Trillions of bytes per second. All we know is when it picks up a lot of keywords at once. Which is what happened. We got 'Jackhammer' several times . . . in Arabic. And the phrase 'Get Ripley' once, also in Arabic. We have a hundred techs working on this right now, going through all that data, trying to find and decrypt the entire message—and hopefully, track it to its source. But that may take a while."

"How long?"

"If we're lucky, hours."

"And if we're not?"

Alexander averted his eyes. "Weeks."

I snapped to my feet. "You mean, I might have to stay down here until then?"

"Of course not," Alexander said in the most soothing voice he could manage. "I assure you, we will find these people long before that."

"When they try to kill me!"

Alexander placed a comforting hand on my shoulder

and steered me back to the couch. "Benjamin, I know this is stressful. I remember the first time *I* was made a target. It was no picnic. But I got through it all right, and you will too. In fact, if you think about this, it's actually quite an exciting opportunity."

"How so?" I asked glumly.

"You've only been here a few weeks and you're already a key part of a real, live mission," Alexander replied. "Do you have any idea how many of your classmates would kill for this chance? And I mean that literally. There are top-quality students out there who've only been running simulations for six years. There are actual *spies* who'll never get to be a part of anything this exciting."

"They'll never get to have assassins target them?" I muttered. "How unlucky for them."

"They *are* unlucky," Alexander said. "None of them have even seen this bunker. They've never had the entire CIA mobilize because of them. And not to sound pompous, but none of them have ever had a chance to work with *me*. Not even my own daughter, and I taught her everything she knows. This is what the Academy of Espionage is all about. This is the brass ring everyone's reaching for—and it's fallen into your hands. It's a once-in-a-lifetime opportunity. Play it right and you just might end up the golden boy here."

And if I play it wrong, I'll end up dead, I thought. But I didn't say it. Because I knew Alexander had a point. When I'd chosen to come to spy school, I'd known I was accepting a potential life of danger. I simply hadn't expected it so soon. Now that it was here, it seemed far less romantic than it had in my imagination . . . but I had to admit, it was kind of exciting, too. "You're right," I finally conceded.

"That's the spirit!" Alexander slapped his knee and laughed. "I'm going to check on our security status. Why don't you make yourself comfortable here? Familiarize yourself with some of this weaponry, fix yourself a drink, grab a magazine. I think there's some cases of snack cakes in the larder. Or, if you want, come on over to the monitoring station and watch us in action."

He trotted back down the hall.

I took his advice and tried to make the best of things. I poured myself a bright green Gatorade and found the snacks. There was a case of Ding Dongs that had been placed down there around 1985, but they had so many preservatives in them, they still tasted like new. I took a pass on examining the weapons—the steel walls of the bunker looked as though they could ricochet an errant bullet around for hours until it ended up in my skull—though I did opt to join Alexander at the monitoring station.

Turns out, it wasn't very exciting.

The monitors merely displayed dozens of static shots of

the perimeter of the school *not* being attacked. The agents kept shifting the images, jumping from camera feed to camera feed, but all were virtually the same. It was like watching the 24-hour Wall Channel. After half an hour I found myself actually *hoping* we'd get attacked. At least then something might happen. As it was, the most thrilling moment was when one of the agents saw a squirrel.

After an hour I chose to go read magazines, many of which hadn't been replaced since the early seventies. I learned quite a lot about the cast of *Bonanza*.

After two hours there was a shift change.

After three hours I was asleep.

After five hours and forty-two minutes, however—at exactly 7:30 in the evening—there was a beep.

It was a persistent and annoying beep, designed to grab your attention but not freak you out, more like a microwave timer than a Klaxon. I came to on the couch and heard excited voices in the monitoring room.

I hurried in and found the agents quickly scrolling through camera feeds while Alexander watched over their shoulders. None of the feeds showed anything but walls and woods, all in night-vision green, as darkness had fallen. No one seemed very concerned, although I did notice sweat on both the younger agents' upper lips.

"What's going on?" I asked.

"We have a breach," Alexander replied. "Southwest perimeter."

I felt my heart begin to race. "Is it the enemy?"

"Friends tend to use the front door, not come over the wall," Alexander said. "Plus, whoever it is, they're crafty. We're having trouble tracking them."

"Got 'em!" one of the agents exclaimed. "Camera 419. Back woods, near the pond."

We wheeled toward his monitor and saw someone in a heavy winter jacket dash through the trees, moving at a full clip. It was impossible to make out any features in the darkness.

"He's coming straight for the school," the other agent said. "Picking him up on Camera 293."

We turned toward his monitor, just in time to see the intruder wing a snowball into the camera lens, blacking it out.

"Is that only one person?" I asked.

"That we can see," Alexander replied. "Which means there's likely a dozen we can't." He snapped out his radio with one hand, his gun with the other. "Attention all agents, this is Big Dog. We have activity in the southwestern quadrant of the property. The enemy has breached the perimeter and appears to be heading for the dormitory. All available agents converge there, on the double." Alexander pointed at the two agents stationed by the door. "Both of you, come with me."

"You're taking my protection?" I asked.

"After we're finished with these guys, you won't *need* any more protection," Alexander said reassuringly. He typed a code into a keypad. The giant door unlocked and slid open.

"But still, it couldn't hurt to leave them behind, right?" I suggested. "Just in case something goes wrong."

"Nothing will go wrong, Benjamin. I'm in charge here." Alexander checked his reflection in the gleaming steel— as though he wanted to make sure he looked good for the troops. "Now let's move out, men. We have an enemy to subdue." He darted down the hall.

The agents who'd been guarding the door dutifully followed him.

I watched the steel door slam closed behind them, then waited for the reassuring click of the dead bolt sliding back into place before returning my attention to the monitors.

Video images were now coming up faster and faster as the agents tried to track everything that was happening on the surface at once. I caught glimpses of the enemy hurtling past cameras in the woods, teams of CIA agents en route to the dormitory, Alexander and the two agents he'd just commandeered racing through the underground tunnels to be part of the action. The radio crackled with inter-agent communications: teams coordinating, requests for intel on the enemy, Alexander ordering everyone to stand down until he arrived.

I saw the enemy race past the gymnasium, closing in on the dorm.

"We have visual," an agent stationed by the dormitory reported.

"Hold all live fire," Alexander told everyone. "If possible, we want these guys alive."

On the monitors I saw Alexander emerge aboveground from two different angles, then fall in with a platoon behind the dorm. There was a quick discussion I couldn't hear, and then the platoon fanned out, ready for action.

The enemy was skirting the mess hall, almost to the dorm, but now something started to bother me. There was something disturbingly familiar about the gait of the man I was watching. And furthermore . . .

"It *really* looks like there's only one guy," I said.

"Yeah," one of the agents at the monitors admitted. "It does."

"Attack!" Alexander ordered.

The monitor screens showed the grounds suddenly coming alive with CIA agents. They emerged from behind buildings, dropped from rooftops, burst out of leaf piles. A dozen nets were launched at once. Four hit their target, while two took out agents who got caught in the cross fire. The enemy went down in a heap, tangled in the nets, then rolled over to find fifty agents converging on him with guns raised.

There was no additional attack from the woods.

Which meant there *was* only one man.

Klieg lights snapped on, bathing the grounds in blinding light. On every monitor the cameras zoomed in on the target. One of them managed to get a shot of his face.

"Oh no," I said.

It was Mike Brezinski.

A second later an explosion blew the steel door off its hinges behind me.

I whirled around to find the room already filling with smoke.

I realized I'd left my weapon in the other room, though it wouldn't have mattered.

Sedation darts took out the agents at the monitors before they could even reach for their guns.

Another nailed me in the shoulder.

The last thing I saw was three hooded men emerging from the smoke, and then darkness closed in.

ABDUCTION

Washington, DC
Streets near the National Mall
February 9
1945 hours

When I came to, I was moving. That was all I could tell for sure. There was a heavy sack over my head that cut out all light, and I was trussed like a calf at a rodeo: My hands were bound behind my back and my ankles were cinched together. I was lying on the floor in the back of a vehicle. I guessed it was a van, because there seemed to be a lot of space, but I couldn't tell for certain. No one had even bothered to buckle me into a seat. I'd merely been tossed inside like a piece of luggage. My shoulder throbbed where the dart had hit me; it felt like I'd been stung by a wasp the size of a Labrador retriever.

I was terrified, but I had the presence of mind to not say anything—or make any sudden movements. For now, it was probably in my best interest to let my abductors think I was still unconscious. Perhaps I could learn something about them that way. When I concentrated, I could detect a faint conversation from the front of the van, though the sound of the road passing through the floor of the vehicle nearly drowned it out. I focused as hard as I could, straining to pick out the words:

"I think the Wizards are going to the play-offs this year," one person said.

"I think you're a moron," said the other.

I frowned. It was the radio.

Though I had to wonder: What foreign terrorist organization listened to American sports radio?

Suddenly, there was an extremely loud *thump* on the roof of the van, as though something had landed on it hard enough to dent the metal.

It startled me—and seemed to have the same effect on my abductors. Someone in the front seat reacted with surprise in a language I didn't know. Then I heard glass breaking, followed by a wet thwack and a few groans.

My fear cranked up a few notches. I had no idea what

was happening. It was possible that someone was trying to rescue me, but it was also possible that another faction of bad guys had just leapt into the mix. This might have been an ambush, a double cross, or a complete and utter screwup. Whatever the case, I was a helpless passenger in a runaway vehicle that dangerous people were fighting for the control of, which was definitely not behavior recommended in driver's ed.

The sounds of a protracted struggle came from the front seat while the van veered wildly. I was pitched from one side to the other while tires squealed beneath me and a cold wind whipped through the shattered window. There was a sudden, bone-rattling jolt as we sideswiped another vehicle. Then two heavy objects—unconscious bodies, I guessed—thudded onto the floor near me. After that came a series of distinct thumps—I wasn't sure how, but I recognized it as the sound of someone's head repeatedly being slammed into a dashboard—and the final thud of a third body landing on the floor. The van swerved uncontrollably for a few more seconds and then finally recovered.

"Hey, Ben," Erica said. "You can stop faking being unconscious now."

I'd never been so happy to hear anyone's voice in my life. "Are we safe?"

"Not quite. But I'm working on it. Hold on."

There was a rattle of machine-gun fire behind us, followed by the sounds of bullets perforating the side of the van.

Our brakes screeched, and the van slewed wildly, as though Erica had purposefully put us into a spin. Gunfire blasted from the front seat, after which I heard the distinct sound of the pursuing vehicle smashing into a wall.

The van stopped skidding and resumed driving normally.

"Okay. *Now* we're safe," Erica said. "At least for a little while."

"Can you untie me?" I asked.

"Give me another minute or so. They're still tracking us."

The van continued on, moving quickly but apparently within the speed limit. I heard police sirens pass us heading in the opposite direction twice—as though racing to the aftermath of what we'd left behind—but no one pulled us over. After five minutes and twenty-three seconds the van slowed and jounced, as though it had suddenly jumped a curb, then stopped.

Five seconds after that, Erica opened the rear doors, dragged me out, and snapped the hood off my head.

The first thing I saw was her face. She was smeared with black camouflage paint and blood, although I couldn't tell if it was hers or someone else's. There was a lump the size of a walnut over her left eye, her lip was swollen, and her hair was a rat's nest, but she still looked gorgeous to me. Of course, it's possible that if a gargoyle saved your life, you'd think it was the most beautiful thing you'd ever seen.

Erica cradled my face in her hands and leaned in. For half a second I thought she was going to kiss me.

Instead, she tilted my head to the side, angled it toward the glow of a streetlamp, and examined my eyes. "Your pupils are slightly dilated," she said. "Looks like they gave you Narcosodex. It's a mild tranquilizer. Feel nauseous?"

"Yes, but I think it's car sickness. I got tossed around pretty good just now."

"Better out than in, just to be on the safe side." Erica jabbed three fingers into my stomach.

I keeled over and threw up.

That was the last thing I ever wanted to do in front of Erica Hale, although I *did* feel considerably better afterward.

While I knelt on the ground, clutching my stomach, I noticed Erica was wearing head-to-toe camouflage gear. It was the winter white variety—to better blend in with the snow—smartly accessorized with a black utility belt. She opened one of the belt's two dozen compartments, removed a small white pellet, and held it out to me.

"Is that a drug that counteracts the tranquilizer?" I asked.

"No, it's a Tic Tac. It counteracts vomit breath."

"I'll take two," I said.

Erica popped them into my mouth, then snapped out a pair of heavy-duty shears and went to work on my bonds.

I wasn't handcuffed. Instead, my wrists and ankles were bound with some sort of flexible wire, so it took Erica the better part of a minute to get through it.

While she did that, I took in my surroundings. We were on the southwest side of the National Mall. The van was parked on a thin strip of land between the road and the Potomac River, about a quarter mile from the Lincoln Memorial, which loomed above the trees to my left like a giant marble air conditioner. To my right, farther away, was the shining dome of the Jefferson Memorial, while ahead of us was a dark expanse of baseball fields and the Tidal Basin. Beyond it, the Washington Monument stabbed into the sky.

I turned around and looked at the van. It was nondescript, dark green with a Virginia license plate I'd bet was stolen. The roof was severely dented and the front windshield was smashed in. The sides were pocked with bullet holes and the paint was gouged a dozen times over. The passenger's side rearview mirror dangled by a wire. If the van had been rented, someone wasn't getting their deposit back.

The men inside the van were in even worse shape. All three were unconscious. Their noses were broken. Their eyes were blackened. Their faces were so lumpy and swollen, it was impossible to tell what they usually looked like.

"What just happened?" I asked.

"I saved your bacon." Erica snipped through the wire binding my ankles and tossed it into the van. Then she pulled something off my rear end and presented it to me. A Post-it note. "This was stuck to your butt. I'm guessing it's theirs. Have any idea what it means?"

All that was on it was a number: 70,200. I shook my head.

Erica secured the Post-it in a plastic evidence bag, then grabbed my arm and tugged me toward the ball fields. "C'mon," she said. "Before their backup arrives."

"Shouldn't we bring one of them?" I pointed to the unconscious bad guys in the back of the van. "Y'know, to interrogate?"

"It's a nice idea, but we don't have the time to lug a body around. This place is gonna be swarming with nasties in two minutes."

I knew better than to argue with her. I turned and ran.

Even though the National Mall in Washington is one of the most popular tourist attractions in the country, it's amazing how little visited some parts of it are. Even on a summer day, when the Lincoln Memorial is thronged with tourists, the southern side of the Reflecting Pool nearby can be virtually empty. On a cold winter night, there wasn't another soul around. A few cars zipped past on Independence Avenue as we darted across it, but otherwise, we might have been miles from civilization.

A large grove of trees ran along the south side of the Reflecting Pool. As we ducked into it, we saw the headlights of three cars stop where we'd left the van. It had taken them slightly under two minutes to arrive. I paused in the cover of the trees to watch, but Erica dragged me on. "Don't stop. It won't take them long to figure out we've come this way. There aren't many other options."

She was right. Between the Potomac and the Tidal Basin, there were few directions for us to have headed that didn't involve swimming. For a moment I thought Erica had made a rare mistake, abandoning the van where she had. She'd left us about as far from cover—or a Metro station—as possible in the city, while the enemy had cars and a lot of men. It wouldn't take them long to catch up with us.

But, as usual, Erica had thought everything out far in advance.

Not far into the woods was a small, almost-forgotten memorial to Chester Alan Arthur, one of our least effective presidents. I'd once stumbled upon it with Mike, a few years before, after a Little League game down on the ball fields. At the time I'd thought it was odd that someone would have bothered to build a monument to Arthur—or that if anyone had really cared, they would have built it where it was doomed to be overlooked by anyone but lost tourists. It was a small monument, marble like everything else in Washington, with a Roman arbor arching over a statue of Arthur, who looked bloated and gassy.

Erica twisted a ring on his finger. A small panel flipped open in the marble, revealing an ancient keypad. Erica entered a code number.

There was a groan, and the statue rotated ninety degrees, revealing a hidden staircase beneath it.

After the events of the night, I hadn't thought anything else could surprise me, but this did the trick. I couldn't believe what I was seeing.

We ducked through the opening, and the statue automatically slid back into place, plunging us into darkness. The stairs descended only one story. Erica hit a switch, lighting a series of bare bulbs that stuck out from the ceiling, revealing a tunnel. It seemed to be significantly older than the tunnels on campus. The walls were stone, rather than cement, and the ceiling was propped up with rotted wood beams, like a mine shaft. It was even colder inside than it was outside.

I began to shiver. I was wearing only a sweatshirt over my clothes.

"Here. Put this on." Erica removed a small packet from another compartment on her utility belt, then unfolded it. It was an ultrathin jacket made of shimmering silver material. "It was developed at NASA for the astronauts."

I pulled on the jacket. It seemed to hermetically seal my body heat around me. Almost instantly, I felt warmer.

We hurried down the tunnel for five minutes until it dead-ended at an ancient iron door. There was no computerized keypad here, only a rusted keyhole. Erica withdrew a key ring from her utility belt and selected a large iron key. It fit the keyhole perfectly. The door swung open with a squeal of protest.

We were now inside a large square room. The walls were made from massive stones, each ten feet across. An iron staircase spiraled up to a trapdoor in the wooden ceiling. It seemed as though we were inside the foundation of a much larger structure.

I calculated how far we must have walked and guessed where we were, but it didn't seem possible. Not until I noticed that many of the stones had inscriptions. One in the corner proclaimed: LAID BY ZACHARY TAYLOR, PRESIDENT OF THE UNITED STATES OF AMERICA, MAY 14, 1849.

"Holy cow," I said. "We're inside the Washington Monument."

"Tell anyone I have the keys and I'll kill you." Erica closed the steel door and locked it from the inside.

"How on earth do you have the keys to the Washington Monument?" I asked. "Did your father give them to you?"

"Don't be ridiculous," Erica laughed. "My *grandfather* did."

She led the way up the staircase. Her key also worked a lock in the trapdoor, allowing us out of the foundation and into the monument itself. We emerged behind a statue of George Washington in a small alcove. The elevator the tourists use was right across from us, but Erica led me through a door to another set of stairs instead.

"We'll have to hoof it," she said, starting to climb. "The elevator makes too much noise. Anyone outside can hear it if they listen closely."

I followed her. The empty shaft soared into the air 555 feet above us. "Why would your grandfather have the keys to the Washington Monument?"

"My family's had the keys since it was built, seeing as it was such an important part of the city's defense system."

"This was built for defense?" I asked, incredulous.

"It's a fifty-story surveillance tower smack in the middle of our nation's capital, constructed on the eve of the Civil War," Erica replied. "You honestly think they built this just for *tourists*?"

"I'm pretty sure everyone in America thinks that," I replied defensively. "Except you." Although, now that we were inside the monument, I could see how Erica's version of the story was possible. Washington, DC, had been burned to the ground in the War of 1812 and then wound up right on the edge of the Northern states during the Civil War. It would have made sense to build something that allowed the military to see the Confederates coming from far away. When the monument was finished, it was the tallest building ever constructed. It did seem the tiniest bit odd that it had all been done solely for sightseeing.

"The whole monument thing was a disinformation campaign to get the public to help pay for this," Erica explained. "There wasn't any income tax in those days. And though the place is outdated technology-wise, it still works just fine. There isn't a better place to observe what's happening on the Mall than up here."

In that instant Erica's plan became clear. I'd been up in the top of the monument several times before, usually on school field trips. It was the perfect place to hide. There were windows facing all directions, which would let us keep tabs on the enemy, and they'd never suspect we were up there.

Still, I couldn't help but be a little afraid. These guys had abducted me from a supposedly impenetrable security chamber less than an hour before. "What if they *do* figure out we're here? Then we'll be trapped."

"They won't figure it out," Erica said reassuringly. "I've been up here at night a million times. No one ever thinks twice about this place."

We continued up the rest of the way in silence. It was hard climbing all the stairs, and even Erica was getting winded. When we reached the top, we went directly to the window that faced west.

The city below us was beautiful at night. The Lincoln Memorial shimmered in the Reflecting Pool, and the lights of Virginia sparkled on the Potomac. If I hadn't been so focused on spotting the enemy, it might have occurred to me that I couldn't have asked for a more romantic place to go with a beautiful girl.

Not that romance ever entered Erica's mind for a second either. "There they are," she said, after barely even glancing out the window.

"Where?" I asked.

"There's three sets of two men. One pair just recovered their buddies from the van. The other two are combing the woods south of the Reflecting Pool for us."

I studied the dark landscape as hard as I could. Now that Erica had brought them to my attention, I could barely make out the two men where we'd abandoned the van. They were bundling their pals into another car, which sped away while I watched. As for the ones hunting us, I couldn't spot any of them. The woods were pure darkness. "How can you see them?" I asked.

"I eat a lot of carrots." Erica watched the woods for

another twenty seconds, then announced, "They've lost our trail. We're safe." She leaned heavily against the wall and gave a tired sigh.

It occurred to me that she'd probably expended a ton of energy rescuing me.

"How'd you find me?" I asked. "When the entire CIA couldn't?"

"I never lost you. I was monitoring everything that was happening. Once every agent on campus starting moving in one direction, I decided to look the other way. Just in case it was a diversion. Sadly, it turned out I was right."

I shook my head. "It wasn't a diversion. The enemy just got lucky. That guy they caught . . . that was my best friend."

Erica's eyes widened. It was perhaps the first time I'd ever seen her surprised by anything. "What the heck was he doing infiltrating the campus?"

"There's a party tonight. He wanted to spring me. But with all the excitement, I forgot to text him back to say no. So he showed up anyhow."

"At exactly the right moment to distract the CIA? That's suspicious."

"Mike Brezinski is not one of the enemy," I said. "I've known him since kindergarten."

"You can't trust anyone," Erica replied.

I tried to change the subject. "What happened after that?"

"While everyone else was surrounding your buddy, the enemy grabbed you. Their mole really came through for them. They knew the whole layout of the school, had the entire underground mapped out. They took you out through the toolshed you followed Chip through the other day, then blew a hole in the wall there. The van was waiting."

"And you followed them?"

"I'd hoped to stop them on campus, but they moved faster than I expected. Luckily, I was able to commandeer a motorcycle and catch up to you."

I stared at her for a second. "And luckily, you actually know how to drive . . . and take out an entire enemy team in a moving van . . . and know the secret entrance to the Washington Monument."

Erica cracked a slight smile, then tried to shrug this off like it was no big deal. "I guess Grandpa taught me a few things."

Something about the comment nagged at me, but I couldn't tell exactly what. An idea was forming in my mind, but it hadn't crystallized yet. I took another glance out the monument window, but I still couldn't spot the enemy in the woods.

"Shouldn't we be calling for reinforcements?" I asked.

Erica shook her head. "Too dangerous. I'm not even carrying my cell phone. The CIA could use it to triangulate our position—and since the Agency's been corrupted, the enemy could find us as well. All we can do is wait for them to give up and go home."

I realized my own cell phone was missing. The enemy had taken it from me. "That's your whole strategy?" I asked, exasperated. "You don't have a backup plan?"

"Like what, exactly?"

"I don't know. Your father's Alexander Hale. Sooner or later, he's bound to notice you're missing, right? You haven't arranged some sort of system with him in case a mission goes wrong?"

Erica sighed. "No. That never really seemed like a good idea."

The idea I'd been struggling with suddenly gelled. It didn't seem right at first, but as I thought back over the events of the evening—as well as every comment Erica had ever made about Alexander—it made more and more sense.

"Your father isn't a very good spy, is he?" I asked.

Erica turned to me, curious. "Why do you say that?"

"*You* suspected there might be a decoy," I replied. "He didn't. In fact, he fell for it so badly, he took my protection, allowing the bad guys to grab me without a fight."

"They still had to take out the agents outside the door. . . ."

"Okay, *less* of a fight. That was a pretty bad mistake for someone who's done as much as Alexander claims he has."

"What do you mean, 'claims'?" Erica asked it the way

one of my professors might have, pushing me to explore the concept further.

"Well . . . your father talks an awful lot about all the great things he's done . . . but I haven't actually *seen* him do anything great. So maybe all your father is *really* great at is convincing everyone how great he is."

"Wow." There was something in Erica's eyes I'd never seen before: respect. "Finally, somebody noticed."

I wasn't sure, but I think I blushed. "You mean, no one else knows?"

"Like who?"

"I don't know . . . the head of the CIA, maybe?"

"If the head of the CIA knew my father was a fraud, do you think he'd have assigned him to protect you?" Erica shook her head. "Alexander has them all snowed: the top brass at the Agency, the staff at spy school, everyone out in the field . . ."

"How could he get away with this for so long?" I asked.

"You hit the nail on the head. He has one talent: making himself look good. And he's exceptional at it. Sometimes he makes up stories, but he usually just takes credit for other people's work."

"And none of the them ever complain?"

"Well, a lot of time they can't, because they're dead." Erica noticed my shock and quickly added, "Oh, Alexander doesn't kill them. Not directly, anyway. He's almost as bad a shot as you are. But quite often people have ended up dead *because* of his incompetence. And yet, somehow, he always manages to sell a story that has him come out smelling like a rose."

"When did you first figure it out?"

"One day, when I was six, my father accidentally blew up our kitchen. He'd just had these missiles installed in the headlights of his car. The trigger was designed to look like one of the radio knobs, but of course, my dad forgot. He was pulling into the garage one afternoon, pressed the wrong button . . . and the next thing you know, all our major appliances are going into orbit."

"Was anyone hurt?"

"No, although my dad's ego took a pretty big hit. And the kitchen was totaled. Our refrigerator ended up in the neighbor's pool. They found the microwave three blocks away." Erica began to giggle. She couldn't control it. It was as though she'd been holding in her emotions for years, but now the dam was breaking. Soon waves of full-on laughter broke loose. "I'm sorry," she gasped. "It's all kind of funny in retrospect. Mom went ballistic. Dad tried to duck the blame, but he was so worked up, he actually claimed that Swedish radicals had sabotaged his car."

I started laughing too. Erica's amusement was infectious. And after days of tension I needed a release myself. "Did he ever screw up anything else?"

"Well, he did single-handedly destroy diplomatic relations between the United States and Tanzania." Erica broke into a new fit of giggles.

"How?" I gasped.

"He was trying to give the president's wife a compliment, but he botched his Swahili and ended up telling her she smelled like a diseased wildebeest."

That was just the beginning. Now that Erica finally had someone to confide in, the stories poured out of her: how Alexander had almost caused the political collapse of Thailand; how he'd triggered a tribal war in the Congo; how he'd come within seconds of initiating a nuclear strike on France. Each tale of his incompetence was more shocking than the last, and yet, through it all, we couldn't stop laughing. (Erica did dead-on impersonations of Alexander, the principal, and everyone else in the intelligence community.) After half an hour I hurt more from laughing than I had hurt after being attacked by ninjas.

I could have happily spent the rest of the night up there, listening to Erica's stories, but sadly, duty called. After relating how Alexander had once lost a briefcase full of military secrets in a Tokyo karaoke lounge, Erica glanced out the window and immediately shifted from being a normal fifteen-year-old girl to the Ice Queen again. "Looks like they're admitting defeat. It's time to go."

The enemy teams had regrouped on the eastern side of the Reflecting Pool by the World War II Memorial. Even I could see them now. They weren't making any attempt to hide; they simply milled among a few other tourists willing to brave the cold. Erica whipped out a pair of binoculars, but they were of no use; the frigid weather gave our enemies an excuse to wrap their faces in scarves.

A van pulled up at the curb. The men jumped in and sped away.

Erica turned to me. "By the way, everything I've told you tonight is completely confidential. Say one word of it and I'll destroy you."

She started for the stairs. But while she was trying to be her usual, distant self, I'd noticed a hint of regret in her eyes. As though she'd wished she could have stayed up there, dishing dirt on her father and laughing for the rest of the night as well.

I followed her down into the dark shaft of the monument. "Have you ever thought of telling all this to someone *important*?" I asked. "Someone who could take Alexander out of circulation before he does any more damage?"

Erica shook her head. "They'd never believe it. My father has covered his tracks too well. And he has friends in very high places. They'd just dismiss it all as the ramblings of a teenage girl with daddy issues. And then I could kiss *my* career good-bye." Erica grew so downcast as she said this, it seemed as if it wasn't mere speculation on her part, but as though she spoke from experience.

"Maybe *you* wouldn't have to share the information," I offered. "Maybe it could come from another source. Like me."

Erica gave me one of her rare, unexpected smiles, but she shook her head. "I don't think it'd work out so well for you, either. Besides, we have bigger fish to fry for now."

I nodded, although with every step toward the bottom of the monument, I grew more reluctant to leave it. First, there was a decent chance the enemy had only *pretended* to leave to lure us out of hiding. But perhaps more significantly, this was the one place Erica had ever felt comfortable opening up to me. I had little doubt that, once we left, she'd shut me out again.

"Where are we going?" I asked.

"Back to campus."

I froze halfway down the stairs. "I was just abducted from campus! From the safest bunker there!"

"That's exactly why we're heading back. You think the director of the CIA would let that happen *twice*? You're gonna have more security than the president."

"Then maybe we should go to the CIA directly. To see the director himself."

"No," Erica said. "We're going to see the one person we can trust."

IMPERSONATION

CIA Academy of Espionage

Faculty Housing

February 10

0200 hours

It took us a long time to work our way back to the academy. We returned via an extremely indirect route, zig-zagging back and forth across the city, using the subway, cabs, and our feet, constantly checking over our shoulders to see if we were being followed.

When we were finally only a block from the campus, I saw to my relief that there were CIA agents posted every-where around it. Three manned the main gate, still alert despite the late hour, guzzling coffee and blowing into their hands to keep warm.

I started toward them, but Erica held me back. "Not so fast."

"What's wrong?" I asked, concerned. "They're on our side, aren't they?"

"Don't look so worried. They're safe. But the moment they see you, they probably have orders to whisk you right off to the principal's office for a debriefing—and all they'll do there is pump you full of lies. If we want the truth about what happened tonight, we'll have to get it ourselves."

We rounded the campus until we came to a bank on the far side of the street. We entered the ATM kiosk, and Erica typed a PIN on one of the machines. Steel curtains instantly dropped over the window, obscuring us from view, and then the ATM swung free from the wall, revealing a hidden staircase beyond. The most surprising thing about this was how unsurprising I found it. At this point, I would have been shocked to enter a building with Erica and *not* find a hidden passageway.

The stairs connected to the maze of subterranean tunnels under the campus, only there was another security door to pass through to access it. "This is the only route from the tunnels that goes off campus," Erica explained. "Thus, it's extremely classified."

"So, of course, *you* know about it," I said.

Erica only smiled in response.

She led me through the underground maze without hesitation, as though she'd committed every hall and intersection of it to memory. Eventually, we climbed a staircase and emerged from behind the snack machine in a building I'd never been inside before. We were in the main lobby of what appeared to be a dormitory, only nicer. The room was cozy and inviting, if a bit threadbare. Leather couches were arranged before a still-smoldering fire. The walls were lined with books. It had the comforting smell of pipe tobacco and weapon lubricating oil.

"Faculty housing?" I asked. Many of the professors still lived at home, though a few were known to have residence at the academy.

Erica nodded, then led me up another flight to a short corridor with only four doors off it. She used her own key to let us into one of them.

The faculty apartments were much nicer than our dorms—although that wasn't saying much. There were prison cells nicer than our dorms. This one was a well-appointed single bedroom with a living room and kitchenette. It was tremendously messy, however, with newspapers strewn everywhere and half-drunk glasses of water teetering on any available surface.

Professor Crandall was asleep in an easy chair in front of the television, wearing a moth-eaten terry-cloth robe over striped pajamas, a racing form across his lap. When we entered, he snapped awake with a start and looked about, disoriented. "Is that you, Thelma?" he asked, sounding more than a little senile. "Back from Tuscaloosa already?"

"You can drop the old coot act," Erica said. "Ripley's cool."

Instantly, Crandall became someone else entirely. His standard slightly confused gaze sharpened, his posture straightened, and he seemed, for the first time in my experience, to know exactly what was going on around him. "Right. I suspect you're here to find out how mucked up everything is, then."

This surprised me. "Hold on," I said. "Your entire personality—the whole doddering professor thing—is an act?"

"Of course." Crandall sounded slightly offended. "The best way to stay in the loop is to let everyone believe you're totally out of it. You have no idea how much information people spill right in front of you when they think you're a drooling idiot. Plus, it throws off your enemies too, and I've racked up my share of those over the years. They tend to underestimate you when they think you're not playing with a full deck." He tossed aside the racing form, revealing the cocked and loaded semiautomatic pistol that had been resting in his lap. "Would either of you care for some tea?"

"I'd love some Orange Zinger if you've got it," Erica said.

"Make it two," I said.

Crandall hopped out of his chair and scooted to the kitchenette. Now that he wasn't putting on an act, he moved like a man fifty years younger, as spry as anyone in my class. "Erica, I assume from your presence here that you've cleaned up after your father again," he asked.

"Yes," Erica replied. "Did anyone important notice?"

"That he royally screwed up?" Crandall said. "Certainly not. He's got the big boys eating out of his hand. One of the agents from the secure room got a bit suspicious, though—Fincher, I think—so your father pinned the blame squarely on him and came out looking pristine, as usual. They'll probably give him another medal for it . . . once they learn Ripley here is alive, of course."

"But they don't know that yet, do they?" I asked.

"No, they don't." Crandall chuckled. "I suspect the higher-ups are all really freaking out right now."

"What's the fallout?" Erica asked.

"Pretty heavy." Crandall plopped tea bags in three mugs. "There's never been an abduction here before. At least three separate internal investigations have been ordered already. And platoons of agents have been mobilized to track down Mr. Ripley. It's like D-day. The head of the CIA bought your little ruse about Jackhammer whole hog and is terrified of what would happen if it fell into the wrong hands. I quite think he's forgotten it was his idea to falsify Ripley's crypto credentials in the first place."

"Then maybe I ought to let them know I'm all right," I said.

"In a rush to be interrogated, are you?" Crandall poured hot water into the mugs. "Because that's what will happen the moment you show your face. You'll be tossed in a holding cell and grilled six ways from Sunday."

I frowned. "Couldn't they just ask me nicely?"

"Perhaps, but this way lets them cover their asses," Erica explained. "The last thing the administration wants is for you to show up here looking like a hero for escaping the enemy and then telling the whole student body the truth about what happened tonight. They need time to do damage control and establish their own version of the story, one in which they don't seem like such idiots that they needed a teenaged girl to rescue you."

"So why don't you rest up first?" Crandall handed me the tea and proffered a plate of homemade chocolate chip cookies as well.

I sampled one. It was easily the best thing I'd eaten at spy school. "This is delicious."

"The secret is, I add a pinch of coconut flakes," Crandall

said proudly. "Now then, it probably behooves us to do a bit of interrogation ourselves. To get an idea of whom we're dealing with here. Can you tell me anything about your abductors, Benjamin? What they looked like, sounded like . . . even smelled like?"

"Not really," I admitted. "I was unconscious with a hood over my head most of the time I was with them. All I know is, they were listening to sports radio. In English."

Crandall cocked a bushy eyebrow, intrigued. "The prevailing theory right now, based upon the chatter that was picked up, is that our enemy is Arabic. Are you suggesting that might be erroneous?"

"Possibly," I said. "Though it's possible that my abductors just like sports. There's not many radio stations here that broadcast in Arabic. And right after Erica jumped on the roof of the van, one of the bad guys spoke in a language I didn't know."

"Could it have been some form of Arabic?" Crandall asked.

"I can't say," I admitted sadly. "I didn't get to hear much. Erica knocked them all unconscious pretty quickly."

"She tends to do that." Crandall gave Erica a pleased smile and seated himself back in his easy chair with a cup of tea. "What about you, dear? What were your impressions?"

"They certainly *looked* Arabic," Erica said. "But I was kind of busy trying not to get killed by them to ask where they were from. Ben's point about the radio is interesting. Maybe they were merely trying to look like Arabs to throw the CIA off their scent. Same goes for broadcasting the chatter in Arabic."

"Why'd they even broadcast the chatter at all?" I asked.

Crandall looked at me curiously. "Do you find something odd about that?"

"Yes," I replied. "Why alert the CIA to the fact that they were coming after me? If they knew the campus so well, why not just sneak in and grab me in the middle of the night?"

Crandall turned to Erica and arched his brows again. "He's smarter than you thought," he said.

Erica shrugged. "He's getting better."

Crandall returned his attention to me. "You make a good point. But consider this: The campus was already crawling with agents. The enemy had a limited amount of time to get you, and they couldn't be sure where you were at any given moment. But with the tip-off, they knew exactly where you'd be: Inside the security room."

"That still doesn't take care of all the agents," I said. "Not unless the enemy *knew* there was going to be a diversion, and they couldn't have possibly known Mike was coming here. *I* didn't even know he was coming."

As I spoke, however, something occurred to me. I didn't do a very good job of hiding it. Crandall and Erica both sat forward.

"What is it?" the professor asked.

"Do you still have that Post-it note?" I asked Erica.

She withdrew it from her utility belt, still in the plastic evidence bag. "This is from the van they used to abduct Ben," she informed Crandall.

I took it from her. There on the Post-it was the number 70,200. Exactly as I'd remembered. I'd simply needed to see it again to make sure my mind wasn't playing tricks on me.

"They *did* know Mike was coming," I said.

Erica sat down next to me. "How can you tell?"

It was the first time I'd known something that she hadn't. I probably should have milked it, but I was in too big of a hurry to impress her. "It's a time. Though, instead of writing it in hours and minutes, they wrote it in seconds. Probably to keep anyone from realizing it's a time. Seventy thousand two hundred seconds after midnight is seven thirty in the evening."

"Exactly the time your friend arrived on campus." Crandall slapped the arm of his chair. "You're positive about that?" He started to do the math on a piece of paper.

"No need for that," Erica told him. "Ben's cryptography skills might be fake, but his math skills are the real deal."

Crandall set down his pencil. "So they plant the chatter and get the CIA to put you right where they want you. Then they tell your friend to come see you at exactly seven thirty to divert the CIA."

"How?" I asked.

"Figure that out and you might just find our mole," Erica said. "We need to talk to your pal."

"Wait. Where *is* Mike?" Even as I asked it, I was angry I hadn't thought of it long before. I'd been so wrapped up in my own plight that night, I'd completely forgotten that my best friend had experienced some terrifying things as well. The last I'd seen of Mike, he'd been staring down the barrel of fifty guns at once. Mike was no stranger to run-ins with authority, but this one still must have scared him stiff.

"Last I heard, he was incarcerated," Crandall said.

"They put him in jail?" I asked, upset.

"No." The professor raised a hand, signaling me to relax. "They're only questioning him. But given the circumstances, I'd say it'll take him quite some time to prove his innocence. For all we know, they're still working on him."

I shuddered, figuring that wouldn't be fun for Mike at all. "And then what happens to him?"

"Probably a full-scale whitewash," Erica said.

"What's that?" I asked.

"They lie to him," Crandall replied. "The most elaborate lie he's ever encountered, to allay any suspicion he has about this place. They'll tell him it really is a science academy, but it was being leased to the Marines for practice and he stumbled across their exercises . . . or there was an FBI sting operation taking place . . . or who knows what. They'll do whatever it takes to sell the story, even drag in the chairman of the armed forces in if they have to."

"And if Mike doesn't buy it?" I knew my best friend well. No one had less respect for authority than he did. I was beginning to think that was a pretty healthy belief system.

Crandall frowned. "Let's just say it's in his best interests to buy it."

I sat forward, worried. "They'll kill him?"

"No," Crandall said. "The people who run the CIA might be incompetent, paranoid, and borderline insane, but they're not psychotic. They'll simply do whatever it takes to make him forget what he's seen. There are several different methods, but none of them is a day at the beach."

I slumped back into my chair, wishing I'd never heard of spy school. It was bad enough that I'd ended up in serious trouble, but at least I'd volunteered for service. Now my best friend had been drawn into danger simply because he wanted to take me to a party at Elizabeth Pasternak's house. He'd tried to do something nice for me—and was suffering for it. I began to understand why Erica kept all human contact to a minimum; her family had been spies long enough for her to know that, if you got close to someone, they could get hurt.

"So the enemy is running circles around the CIA," I

234 · STUART GIBBS

said, "And instead of doing something about it, they're busy working over Mike."

"Oh, it's worse than that," Crandall said. "They're considering initiating Project Omega."

I had never seen Erica look truly concerned about anything until that moment. She wheeled on Crandall, eyes wide. "Because of *this*? Why?"

"Because they're scared," Crandall told her.

"Hold on," I interrupted. "What's Omega?"

"The last-ditch, end-of-the-line program," Erica said bitterly. "They shut down the academy."

"They can't do that!" I said. Given how upset I'd been at spy school a minute before, I was surprised by how much I hated the idea of it being closed. Maybe the place wasn't for me, but without it, where was someone like Erica supposed to go? And how would I ever see her again?

"Sure they can," Erica replied sourly. "One mole can corrupt decades of work. It doesn't matter how good I am. If my name gets leaked, I'm useless as a spy. Same goes for everyone else here. So why even bother to keep the place open any longer? It's just a waste of money. . . ."

"Now, now," Crandall said reassuringly. "You're acting like the decision has already been made."

"Well, why wouldn't they initiate Omega?" Erica asked. "The enemy has already shown they know this campus inside and out. They kidnapped Ben out of the security room! How much more compromised could the place be?"

"I'll admit, it looks bad," Crandall said. Then he added pointedly, "However, the higher-ups aren't meeting to discuss Omega until this afternoon. If some significant progress could be made in the mole hunt before then, maybe that'd color their thinking."

"How significant?" I asked.

"We'd need to find the mole." Erica turned to Crandall. "What time's the meeting?"

"One o'clock," the professor replied. "Right here, in the main conference room."

"Where's that?" I asked.

"In the Hale Building, next to the library," Crandall told me.

I checked my watch. It was two thirty in the morning. We had fewer than twelve hours to catch a mole who'd outfoxed the entire CIA the night before. It didn't seem possible.

Erica was undaunted, however. She was now revved up, determined to do anything she could to save the academy. "What's our best lead?" she asked.

It took me a moment to realize she was asking *me*, not Crandall. I scrambled to make sense of everything that had happened in the last day. One name sprang to mind before all others. "Uh . . . Chip Schacter."

"Chip?" Crandall laughed. "That boy's a moron."

"Or maybe he just wants us to *think* he is," I said, which struck home with Crandall and silenced him quickly. "He wanted me to meet him a few hours ago." I found the crumpled note in my pocket and showed it to the others: *Meet me in the library tonight. Midnight. Your life depends on it.*

Erica read it, then looked at me, surprised. "That's Chip's handwriting, all right. Why didn't you mention this?"

"It sort of slipped my mind," I replied. "What with being abducted by the enemy and all."

"Any idea what this was about?" Erica asked.

"No," I admitted.

Crandall set his teacup down with a sigh. "No offense, Benjamin, but this isn't much of a lead. . . ."

"Chip's connected to the last bomb that was under the school," Erica said. "Either he planted it or he found it. That puts him closer to the plot than anyone else. And now he's reaching out to Ben."

"If this note is even from him," Crandall cautioned. "Handwriting's not hard to fake. This could be a wild-goose chase, designed to cost us valuable time."

"There's one other thing about Chip," I said. "He's dating Tina Cuevo."

Erica and Crandall both wheeled on me, surprised by the information—and the fact that I knew it before they did.

"How do you know that?" Erica asked.

I started to answer, but Crandall suddenly put a finger to his lips, signaling me to be quiet.

In the ensuing silence I heard the distant sound of feet coming up the main stairwell. It was so faint, it was amazing Crandall had picked it up while we were talking.

Crandall flicked on his television. It appeared to be ancient, but it was actually linked to the campus security system. Crandall quickly found the camera feed from the stairs in the building. Six men were ascending, armed to the teeth.

"The enemy!" I gasped.

"Worse," Crandall said. "The administration." He spun toward us. "If they catch you, your investigation is over. Go! Find Chip!"

Erica already had the window open.

I followed her out it. After the warmth of Crandall's apartment, the cold air hit me like a slap in the face. I leapt the one story to the ground.

They were waiting for us outside. The building was surrounded.

A dozen lights snapped on at once, blinding me. Dark shapes raced at me from the shadows. "Ripley!" one shouted. "Don't run! We just want to make sure you're all right!"

"Don't listen to them!" Erica warned me as she leapt into action, a flurry of kicks and whirls. Several of her attackers went down quickly, clutching various body parts and groaning in pain. But there were too many for her to save me, too.

Now that she'd gone on the attack, the agents dropped any pretense of concern for my well-being and swarmed me. I did my best to escape, but that wasn't much. I only managed to knock one man's glasses askew before the others piled atop me. Through the tangle of arms and legs, I caught a glimpse of Erica disappearing into the woods with a horde of agents behind her.

Then someone shoved my face into the ground and hissed in my ear. "Come with us. The administration wants to speak to you."

INTERROGATION

Cheney Center for the Acquisition of Information
February 10
1200 hours

I spent the next nine hours in an interrogation chamber.

In the movies they always make interrogation rooms look like cold, terrible places, small cement cells furnished with only steel chairs and a one-way mirror that everyone *knows* is a one-way mirror. At the academy, the interrogation rooms were still terrible places, but at least they were comfortably furnished. Mine had a plush couch, sisal carpeting, and a small Zen fountain. New age music played from a hidden speaker. It was like being in the waiting room at a spa—all the better to lull someone into spilling their guts, I suppose.

A succession of agents paraded through, each trying to find out what I knew. They were of all ages, shapes, and ethnicities, and they tried every interrogation approach in the book. (There actually *was* a book: *Mattingly's Advanced Methods of Interrogation.* I had to read it for my Information Acquisition seminar.) Mostly, these were intended to be variations on the "good agent/bad agent" routine, although "incompetent agent/even less competent agent" was a more appropriate description. Only a few of them seemed remotely interested in what I knew about the enemy. Most were far more concerned about my own loyalties, as though *I* were the real problem.

The main sticking point was that no one believed what had actually happened: that I had single-handedly been rescued from the enemy by a fellow student—and a fifteen-year-old girl at that. No one doubted that Erica was incredibly competent; they had her file on hand, although not Erica herself. She'd not only escaped but also continued to elude them, which should have served as further evidence of her competence, but which instead made them question *her* loyalties as well. What made much more sense to all of my inquisitors was that I was somehow in cahoots with the enemy, and that they'd purposely freed me as part of some complicated scheme.

"How, exactly, did Erica engineer your escape?" I was asked time and time again.

"Why didn't you attempt to contact us after you got away?"

"What did you do instead?"

"What is your relationship with Miss Hale?"

"Do you love America?"

"What's that have to do with anything?" I asked.

"Just answer the question," my interrogator said.

So I did. I answered it and every other question truthfully—though, inevitably, someone else would enter the room and ask them all over again.

I also talked to a lot of people who acted like agents but whom I guessed were actually lawyers. They all seemed concerned that, if I were truly innocent, then I might want to sue the academy for gross negligence (i.e., allowing me to be captured and then failing to recover me). I was asked to sign dozens of forms filled with confusing legal jargon. I didn't sign a single one.

Instead, I consistently pressed everyone to stop asking me questions and giving me forms to sign and just *listen to me.* Chip Schacter had to be tracked down. If anyone needed to be interrogated, it was *him.* He was seeing Tina Cuevo. Tina Cuevo was the only student who'd been given my original file—*and* the only student Erica had copied on the e-mail about Jackhammer. Chip could have easily accessed that information through Tina and passed it on to the enemy. Or maybe Tina had passed the information on herself. Whatever the case, there was a reason to investigate them.

Virtually everyone ignored me. The only one who didn't was a stout, red-faced woman with hair so shellacked, it looked bulletproof. And she didn't really listen so much as take offense.

"Are you telling us how to run our investigation?" she asked angrily.

"I'm trying to pass on information," I said. "I thought that was the whole point of this interrogation."

"Because it sounds to me like you're telling us," she snapped. "You. A first-year student. Who doesn't know squat about spying. Why don't you leave the investigating to the professionals?"

"Last time I tried that, I got kidnapped," I replied.

The woman turned an angry shade of red, then stormed out of the room.

No one came in for a long time after that. They didn't want me to know how long it actually was, because there were no clocks in the room and they'd confiscated my watch. I think it was some sort of interrogation tactic, though it's possible they had no idea what to do with me. For a while I shouted at the people on the other side of the one-way mirror that they were squandering precious time, but when no one responded, there was nothing for me to do except sit on the couch and make a show of being annoyed.

Eventually, after what seemed like hours, the door opened and Alexander Hale entered.

Even though my image of Alexander had paled greatly over the past day, he was still a sight for sore eyes. He wore a custom-tailored gray suit with a crisp white pocket square. Instead of sitting down, however, he held the door open and glanced at the one-way mirror furtively. "Come on, Ben. Let's move."

I didn't need to be told twice. I sprang to my feet and followed him. It wasn't until we were outside the room, in what I recognized as the complex of tunnels beneath campus, that I dared ask, "Am I free to go?"

"Not exactly," Alexander said. "But as far as I'm concerned, you are. I asked for some time with you man-to-man. Off the record. No observers."

"So you're springing me? Won't you get in trouble for that?"

"Let's just say I owe you one. And besides, Erica says you're more help out than in." Alexander led me through the tunnels quickly, even running when there was no one around to see us, until we arrived back at the secret ATM entrance Erica had showed me the night before. He opened the door to the secret stairwell, but only waved me through.

"You're not coming?" I asked.

"I have to go back and cover your tracks." Alexander gave me a fatherly pat on the cheek. "But don't worry. You're in good hands."

Before I could say another word, he shut the door behind me.

I rushed up the stairs and emerged from behind the ATM into the fake bank kiosk. Then I stepped out the door onto the sidewalk—and just like that, I was free. The stone wall of the academy loomed across the street, but I was on the other side of it.

"Welcome back, Ben," Erica said.

I started in surprise before realizing the voice was coming from inside my head. Alexander had slipped a two-way radio into my ear.

There were lots of people out and about. The enemy had taken my cell phone, but I put my hand to my ear and pretended to be talking on one anyhow. No one gave me a second glance. Virtually everyone else was on a cell phone themselves. "Can you hear me?" I asked.

"Loud and clear," Erica replied.

"Where are you?"

"Still on campus, looking into things. But I need you to tail someone for me."

"Chip?"

"No. I think he's clean."

"What? But—"

"I'll explain later. Right now I need you to go after Tina. She's the mole . . . and she's on the move."

AMBUSH

Washington, DC

Streets in proximity to the Academy of Espionage

February 10

1230 hours

Erica informed me Tina was on her way out the front gate of the academy, so I hurried around the campus perimeter, racing to beat her there. I held up a block from the gate and fell in with a small group of people waiting for a bus.

Two limousines with diplomatic license plates came down the street and turned through the academy gate. The agents posted there saluted and waved them through.

"Looks like the higher-ups are arriving to discuss Omega," I said.

"Oh, yeah. It's a regular Who's Who in Espionage here today," Erica replied. "We've got the directors of the CIA, FBI, and NSA; the congressional chairs of the Intelligence Committee; a couple White House liaisons; and, of course, no party would be complete without my father. . . . Okay, here comes Tina."

Tina Cuevo emerged through the gate a second later, swaddled in a chic overcoat with a wool cap yanked tightly over her head. She looked around cautiously, though I didn't know if this was because she was afraid of being followed or because it was merely a reflex for anyone in her final year of spy school. Whatever the case, she didn't notice me and hurried across the street.

"Give her a half block and then follow her," Erica instructed. Apparently, she knew that while I'd studied tailing someone, I'd never done it. Our field tests in clandestine pursuit weren't scheduled until spring.

I did exactly as I was told.

Tina moved quickly through the streets of the city, checking her watch each minute or so, as though she was on a tight schedule. Every now and then, she fired a cursory glance over her shoulder, but these were so quick, I don't think she would have noticed me unless I was wearing a gorilla suit. I felt comfortable enough to talk to Erica on my "phone." "Any idea where she's going?"

"No, but she got a text and bolted all of a sudden. And not long before the meeting started. That's suspicious."

"Suspicious enough to think she's the mole?"

"Oh, I've got more on her than that. Courtesy of Chip."

"Chip?"

"Yeah. After I shook the goon squad, I tracked him down and asked him what he wanted to talk to you about last night. Turns out, he was coming to you for help."

"Me?!" I failed to conceal my surprise. "I've only been here for a few weeks. Why not you?"

"Apparently, I intimidate people. He was worried I'd turn him in."

"For what?"

"Doing an unauthorized investigation. Chip didn't plant that bomb under the school. He was trying to figure out who did."

Tina scurried across a street right before the light changed. I got caught on the wrong side of traffic and had to dodge a few cars to get across safely.

"Why didn't he just go to one of his professors?" I asked.

"On the one hand, he wasn't sure it *was* a bomb. A real one, at least. He thought it might be a test. That's the type of quality paranoia four years of spy school instills in you. On the other hand, Chip feared that, if the bomb *was* real, and his first reaction was to merely tell someone else, the administration might consider him ineffectual."

"Even though that might save lives?"

"This is Chip we're talking about. He's used to getting someone else to do his thinking for him. Which is why he reached out to *you*. He respected that you didn't rat him out to the principal."

"I didn't rat him out because he *threatened* me not to."

"Again, this guy isn't exactly Albert Einstein. He was also really impressed when you mouthed off to authority. He thought you were trying to toady up to him."

Tina ducked into a bank. We were now six blocks from campus. It was a normal, everyday bank, too small for me to follow her inside without her noticing me. So I posted myself outside the window and watched as Tina stood in the teller line.

"She's gone into a bank," I reported.

"To do what?"

"I don't know. She's just waiting for the teller."

"I don't suppose you have a scope on you?"

"Sorry. They confiscated everything. I don't even have a phone. I'm pretending to talk into my hand."

"Okay. Keep an eye on her."

"So what'd Chip have to say?" I asked.

"That he's not the mole. Tina is."

"And you just took his word for it?"

"Of course not. What am I, an amateur? I grilled him pretty hard. But whoever your source was got things wrong. Chip isn't seeing Tina. He's been *investigating* her."

"And Chip was right?"

"Well, he can't be a *total* idiot. After all, he got into spy school."

And I didn't, I thought. "What'd he have on her?"

"A good amount of evidence. Hard stuff: e-mails, photos, and such. Tons of it. I haven't had time to go through it all, but I think he can prove she planted the bomb downstairs. Plus, he's got some other circumstantial stuff. I'm following up on it."

"Where? You're breaking up." The radio connection was weakening, interrupted by bursts of static.

"I'm in the tunnels under the Hale Building. I've got an idea what the enemy is up to."

Before I could ask Erica what that was, someone grabbed me from behind.

I whirled around, ready for a fight.

Mike Brezinski was standing there. He leapt back from me, not so much afraid of my fists as still skittish after being swarmed by CIA agents the night before. "Whoa! It's just me!" he exclaimed.

I was thrilled to see he was all right—and yet his presence there was unnerving as well. "What are you doing here?" I asked.

"I wanted to talk to you," Mike said.

"What'd you do? Tail me from campus?"

"Yeah. 'Cause last time I tried to see you *on* campus, I nearly got shot to bits."

"Ben, you can't have your friend around right now," Erica warned. "He'll tip off Tina. You need to shake him."

"I know," I said, completely forgetting that I wasn't supposed to answer Erica when someone else was around.

"You did?" Mike thought I'd been responding to him. "How?"

"Uh . . . I can't talk about it right now," I said sadly. "This isn't a great time. . . ."

"Did you hear me?" Mike demanded. "I nearly got killed last night! Because I tried to spring you for a party!"

"I know," I said again. "And I'm sorry. But they've had some security issues on campus, and I guess the patrol got a little overzealous."

"Aw, Ben, give me a little credit," Mike snapped. "Those jerks tried to force-feed me that line a hundred times over last night. Now, I played dumb with *them* so they'd let me go. But I'm not doing that with you. I mean, honestly, I don't care how bad the crime is, nobody gives their neighborhood watch night-vision goggles. Those guys were professionals, right?"

"Right," I admitted. There no longer seemed to be any point in lying.

"What part of 'shake this guy' did you not understand?" Erica asked me.

While I knew Erica was right, I couldn't bring myself to ditch Mike. He'd been used and practically traumatized because of me, and I felt horrible about it. Besides, Tina seemed to be in a protracted conversation with her bank teller and wasn't going anywhere soon.

"This isn't a normal science school, is it?" Mike asked.

I wasn't quite sure how to answer that with Erica able to hear everything, so I tried to deflect the question. "What'd they do to you?"

"You mean *after* they nearly killed me? Well, they didn't even apologize, for starters. Instead, they stuck me in a room with new age music and a cheap one-way mirror and grilled me like a steak until the middle of the night. And even though I played dumb, they still didn't cut me loose until after one in the morning. Then they drove me home and ratted me out to my parents. So not only did I miss the Pasternak party, I also got grounded."

"Then how are you here right now?"

"How else? I'm ditching school."

"Aw, Mike, I'm really sorry."

"So you've said. But are you really?"

"What?" I asked, shocked by the accusation. "Why would you say that?"

"Because ever since I got busted trying to spring you last night, you've totally blown me off," Mike replied. "I've called you, texted you, e-mailed you . . . and you ignored all of it."

"I haven't had my phone and—"

"And you totally gave me the slip last night."

I'd been trying to keep one eye on Tina, but now I directed all my attention to Mike. "When?"

"Right outside campus. I saw you from the car as I was leaving. You and some hot chick were going into an ATM vestibule. I called out to you, but you completely ignored me."

I groaned, realizing what had happened. Even though the campus had been swarming with CIA agents the night before, none of them had spotted me. My own best friend had. That's how they'd known Erica and I had returned. The only reason it had taken the agents so long to find us was because they never suspected we'd go to Crandall's.

"Mike, I swear, I didn't hear you," I said.

Mike raised his hands, backing off. "All right. I'll give you that one. I can see why that girl would command your full attention. Was that Erica?"

"How's he know my name?" Erica asked, suspicious.

"How do you know her name?" I asked.

"Dude, you *told* me," Mike said. "On the phone a few weeks ago. You bragged that she'd snuck into your room after curfew."

"You told him that?" Erica sounded upset.

"It wasn't a dating thing," I said quickly. "She only wanted to work on a project together."

"That's not how you made it sound *then*," Mike said with a laugh. "And frankly, that's not how it looked last night. The two of you are sneaking around campus together at one thirty in the morning, but you're not dating? Ben, own this. You should be proud! When you told me Erica was hot, I thought you were blowing smoke, but you were right. That girl is on fire!"

"Ben, we need to talk," Erica said coldly.

"So have you kissed her yet?" Mike asked.

I looked back toward the bank, hoping Tina would be leaving. I was desperate for *anything* to interrupt the conversation. A gunfight would have been preferable to having Erica overhear another sentence. Thankfully, Tina was heading toward the door.

"Mike," I said, "I'm not seeing her. Really."

Mike's mood shifted from excited to hurt. "I can take those jackbooted thugs lying to me, Ben. But you're my *friend*. Or, at least, you used to be. But you haven't been acting like one ever since you came to this stupid school."

"It's complicated. . . ."

"No, it's simple: You're being a jerk. You're lying to me. You're ignoring me. And you're totally yanking me around."

"I'm not!" I protested.

"You told me to come spring you last night, and then you completely abandoned me when I got in trouble."

Tina was exiting the bank with a package under her arm. I knew I was supposed to follow her, but I turned back to Mike instead. "Wait. What do you mean *I* told you to come spring me?"

"You texted me!"

"No, I didn't."

"What do you call *this*, then?" Mike pulled out his phone and started searching for something on it.

Tina was about to round the corner and disappear from my sight.

I expected Erica to chastise me for not following her, but Erica seemed to be distracted by something on the other end of the radio link.

So I stayed put. It was a judgment call, based on something Erica had told me earlier that morning: If we learned how the enemy had manipulated Mike, we might catch the mole. Now Mike was claiming that *I* had sent him critical text, when I hadn't. Figuring out what had happened suddenly seemed like the key to everything.

Mike found what he was looking for and thrust the phone into my hand. "There you go. Cold, hard proof."

He was right. There was a text from my phone.

In for the party. Come spring me. 7:30 p.m. on the nose.

Explicit directions followed. The precise location to jump the wall. What route to take to the dormitory. A warning to avoid the cameras. Everything to set Mike up as a patsy.

And the exact time it was sent: 1:23 p.m.

For once, my ability to always know what time it was had a practical application. I knew *exactly* what I'd been doing at 1:23 p.m. the day before. And thus, I knew who'd used my phone.

Everything clicked into place. I suddenly understood what the enemy's plan was.

I didn't have to follow Tina anymore. Just like Mike, she'd been used as a patsy. A distraction from what was really important.

Which meant I had to get back to campus as fast as possible.

I thrust Mike's phone back into his hands. "I'm really sorry. But I have to go. I promise, I'll make this up to you. You're my best friend. That's more important to me than anything."

"Whoa." Mike took a step back, uncomfortable with all the emotion. "Apology accepted. No need to get all mushy. What's the emergency?"

"I have to find Erica," I said.

"Then why are you still here?" Mike grinned wolfishly. "Go get her, Tiger."

I bolted down the street, racing back toward the academy. I was in too big a hurry to even pretend to speak into my imaginary phone.

"Erica!" I said. "I know who the mole is!"

She didn't respond. Instead, I heard a sharp smack and then the distinct groan of Erica collapsing, unconscious.

REVELATION

CIA Academy of Espionage

Subbasement Level 2

February 10

1300 hours

I used the secret entrance through the ATM portal to get back on campus. I'd considered going straight through the front gate and recruiting the agents posted there to help me, but I was afraid they'd only incarcerate me again. I had taken the underground route enough times lately that I was starting to learn it and got lost only once on my way.

I knew I was being careless, rushing headlong to confront the enemy. I knew I should find someone to back me up, but I wasn't sure whom to trust and without my phone,

I had no idea how to locate anyone without wasting precious time. There wasn't even time for me to visit the armory and get a weapon. It always took at least five minutes to fill out a firearms request form, which was five minutes I didn't have. Right then, every second counted.

Erica had told me she was under the Nathan Hale Building. I wasn't sure where exactly, but I guessed she'd been snooping directly under the conference room, as that's where the meeting about Project Omega was taking place. Every major player in American espionage was there. With a single bomb, the enemy could take them all out at once.

But where was it? There were two levels below the library—and those were only the ones I *knew* about. It was possible there might have been another ten down there. And each level was a warren of tunnels, shafts, and locked rooms. I wasn't even sure exactly where the conference room was in the Hale Building, which was a massive edifice, the biggest on campus, with a footprint the size of a football field. There might have been a thousand places to conceal a bomb beneath it.

As I neared the Hale Building, however, I heard a faint beeping in my ear. It was coming from the transmitter, and it grew slightly louder with every step I took.

Erica, I thought. She must have triggered some sort of tracking system before she was knocked unconscious. It obviously only worked within close range, but that was all I needed. I let the beeping lead me through the tunnels, down to Subbasement Level 2, until I found myself outside a steel door marked FURNACE ROOM. The beeping was so loud there, I had to take the transmitter from my ear.

There was a maintenance closet across the hall. The door was locked but flimsy. It took only three kicks to smash it in.

The shelves were loaded with industrial cleaners—the perfect things for me to make a chemical weapon out of— if I had taken Chemistry 105: Constructing Weapons from Cleaning Supplies yet. As it was, I had to opt for something a bit more basic: I snapped a mop handle over my knee, turning it into a club with a relatively sharp end. Then I went back across the hall.

The furnace room door wasn't locked. It creaked softly as it opened, but the sound was swallowed up by that of the huge, ancient furnace, which clanked and chugged noisily as it struggled to heat the building above.

Erica lay unconscious against one wall, a small trickle of blood oozing from behind her ear.

Along the opposite wall sat the bomb. It looked like the bomb I'd seen Chip with in the tunnels before, only several hundred times larger. The block of C4 explosive was the size of a filing cabinet, big enough to level the Hale Building. A maze of wires extended from it, all leading up to a digital alarm clock, which was currently being rigged as a trigger . . .

By Murray Hill.

He had his back to me, but I knew it was him. I'd known since the moment I saw the message on Mike's phone. It had been sent at the exact time Murray had gone off to get pie the day before.

He'd swiped my phone from my jacket, sent Mike the text, then deleted the outgoing message from my text log. It wouldn't have been hard to do. He would have needed my access code, but that probably hadn't been hard to get. I must have carelessly entered it in front of him at some point in the past few weeks, thinking he was actually my friend. All Murray had to do was keep his eyes peeled and remember it. Once he'd set up Mike as the diversion, he'd notified an associate to plant the chatter, gotten some pie, and slipped the phone back in my jacket. Then, after Alexander had removed me from the mess hall, Murray had gone off to arrange my kidnapping.

The only thing he couldn't do was delete the text from Mike's end. But he'd most likely assumed that Mike would never show me the text on his own phone—or that by the time he did, the Hale Building would already be a smoking hole in the ground.

From what I could tell, Murray hadn't finished rigging the bomb yet, although I couldn't be sure. I didn't know much about bombs, though I did know one key thing about Murray: You couldn't trust a single thing about him.

I cocked the mop handle over my shoulder like a baseball bat and crept up on him, focusing on the sweet spot at the back of his skull—the same place he'd probably brained Erica—intending to clobber him with all my might and knock him unconscious. The clanking furnace covered the sound of my footsteps as I closed the gap. . . .

"I wouldn't do that if I were you, Ben." Murray didn't even turn around. Instead, he held up his left hand, in which he clutched a pressure-release trigger. "If you knock me out, I drop this . . . and kablooey."

"Back away from the bomb," I said, in as threatening a voice as I could muster.

"Sure. Just give me one more second. Ah! There we go." Murray plugged a final wire into the digital clock and turned to face me with a smile. "Why don't you put that weapon down so we can have a civilized discussion? C'mon, I'll buy you an ice cream." He started for the door.

"Stop or I'll hit you," I said.

Murray froze and gave me an annoyed look. "No, you won't. You'd just blow up everyone—including yourself. You don't want that."

"I'd also blow *you* up," I pointed out. "And *you* don't want that. So it looks like we're stuck here."

"Not exactly." Murray withdrew a gun from beneath his jacket and aimed it at my stomach. "Gun beats stick. I win." He casually tossed aside the pressure-release trigger, which turned out to be a useless piece of junk. Like I said, you could never trust him.

He was now too far away for me to hit him with my mop handle. I lowered it, defeated, glaring hatefully at him.

"Don't look at me like that," he said. "If I wanted to shoot you, I'd have shot you already."

"Then why haven't you?" I asked.

"Because I have a business proposition for you." He motioned me toward the door with the gun. "Mind if we discuss it somewhere more comfortable than this? I wasn't kidding about that ice cream."

"I'd rather stay here," I said.

"I'm paying. You can even get sprinkles."

"The last time you got me dessert, it was a ruse to arrange my abduction."

Murray sighed, exasperated. "You realize that's a bomb over there, right? Now, it doesn't go boom unless I say it goes boom, but still, the farther we get from it, the safer we are."

"You want to talk to me, then talk." I wasn't sure why I felt it was necessary to stay in the room, but it seemed that if I left, I'd lose any chance I had to prevent the explosion. Or rescue Erica. "What's this proposition?"

"How'd you like to be a double agent?" Murray asked.

Even though I'd been expecting him to do something to catch me by surprise, this completely floored me. "You're offering me a job?"

"*I'm* not doing it. My superiors are. They've seen your file, of course. I leaked it to them. And they like what they see . . . even though we all know the whole cryptography specialist thing is a crock."

"I figured as much." I did my best to sound reverential, hoping it would get him to drop his guard. "You've merely been playing along with that to set up Scorpio all along, right? First you make it obvious to the CIA that there's a double agent at the school. You leak some information. Send an assassin to my room to prove you can infiltrate the campus. Then when Erica plays the Jackhammer card, you have your boys kidnap me. All just to frighten the government into considering the activation of Omega. Because you know only a crisis like that would bring all the higher-ups in espionage together at one time, which makes it the perfect opportunity to take them all out."

"You figured that all out yourself?" Murray asked. He sounded impressed, but he might have been faking it as well. "I *knew* I was right about you. That's the kind of clever deductive thought we're looking for."

"Oh, I've figured out more than that," I replied. "You've

been manipulating everyone left and right. For example, you pretended to let it slip that Chip was seeing Tina to divert my attention to him, but really, *you're* the one who's been using her." I remembered the tutoring manuals I'd seen stacked in Tina's room. "You didn't flunk your classes last semester so you could get a desk job. You did it so Tina would tutor you."

Murray grinned. "Guilty as charged."

"That's how you got your information. You swiped it from her. But then, when Chip—of all people—started to realize a bomb plot was afoot, you just deflected his attention toward Tina herself."

Murray shrugged. "I admit that was a little sloppy. But let me tell you, it is not easy to sneak this much explosive material into a CIA facility. I dropped a little down in the tunnels. Thankfully, it was that lummox who found it and not someone intelligent."

"You did make one mistake, though," I said.

"What?"

"You actually *like* Tina. So you asked her to run an errand for you today so you could get her off campus before the bomb exploded."

"I wasn't doing that to protect Tina." Murray rolled his eyes. "I was doing that to get *you* off campus. I wasn't planning on having this conversation until after the big kaboom, but you caught on faster than I expected. I tell you, you're gonna make an awesome double agent."

"How long have you been doing it?" I asked. "Were you already a plant when you started here?"

"No. Remember when I said I used to be just like you, but then someone showed me the light? That was my recruiter. A very successful double agent in the CIA. He turned me around this time last year."

"Who do you work for?" I demanded. "The Saudis? The Russians? Jihadists?"

"Better," Murray replied proudly. "You know how America is now outsourcing its peacekeeping, hiring independent contractors to handle part of it? Well, the bad guys are doing the same thing."

I took a step back, stunned. "The bad guys are outsourcing evil?"

"Well, we don't refer to it as 'evil' per se, but yes. I work for an international consortium of independent agents who cause chaos and mayhem for a price. A very good price. We're called SPYDER."

"Why?"

"'Cause it sounds cool. And frankly, calling ourselves 'an international consortium of independent agents who cause chaos and mayhem for a price' is a mouthful."

I was shocked by how blasé he seemed about everything.

It was as though he were discussing an after-school social club rather than a criminal organization that had enlisted him to plot the deaths of dozens of people. "Do you even know who contracted you to do this?" I asked.

Murray shrugged again. "What's it matter, as long as the checks clear? Now, I know what you're thinking: I'm a callous and selfish jerk. Well, it's true. I used to be a Fleming like you, only wanting to do good in the world. But then I learned that, even if *you* always want to do the right thing, it doesn't mean the people you're working for do. The fact is, *nobody's* good. I mean, yeah, a couple people are . . . but organizations aren't. Governments aren't. Look at good old America, bastion of democracy and freedom, right? Except for all the coups we've funded in the third world, the useless wars we've waged, and the environmental degradation we've caused. Look at this academy itself. How has this place treated *you*? It's used you as *bait*. Lied to you from day one. Made you a pawn. Hung you out as a target for the enemy . . ."

"But *you're* the enemy!" I protested.

"And we never killed you, even when we had the chance," Murray said. "Now, think about how much better we'll treat you when you *work* for us. Know what you'll make as a CIA agent, traipsing around third world cesspits, doing the dirty work for politicians? Diddly-squat. SPYDER, on the other hand, pays very well. And it's all under the table, totally tax-free. Most of our employees retire as multimillionaires before they're forty. Of course, you have to fake your own death first to throw everyone off your trail, but then you can spend the rest of your life in luxury on a tropical island. How's that sound?"

"Pretty good," I admitted. I wasn't faking that part. Except for the evil bits, Murray had a lot of valid selling points. "How would I fit in?"

"Oh, this is the perfect time to join up," Murray said. "Most double agents start on the ground floor, like I had to, working as a mole in spy school. But after today, once we behead every espionage organization simultaneously, the American spy complex is going to be in chaos. They won't know which end is up for months! And SPYDER has highly placed operatives in positions of power all through the government who'll have even more power after today. We could swing you internships at the CIA, the FBI, or the Pentagon, all with access to highly classified and sensitive material. Or get you a summer job as a page in the Capitol. Or, dare I say, the White House. And from there, who knows how high you can go? SPYDER's been talking about getting a double agent president in office for some time now. Maybe it could be you. The world can be your oyster, Ben. All you have to do is say yes."

Murray lowered his gun slightly and looked at me expectantly.

I carefully thought over everything he'd said.

"Yes," I said.

"Really?" Murray looked thrilled.

"Really," I repeated. "You're right. This place has treated me like garbage." I wasn't *really* interested in SPYDER; I was only faking it to get Murray to drop his guard. But the frustrations I had with spy school were genuine. I could barely contain them. "They brought me in as bait, knowing I could get killed, and didn't even have the decency to tell me. I've been set up, humiliated, bullied, locked in the Box, and attacked by ninjas. They let me get captured, and then—when I escaped—they acted like *I* was the bad guy. If this is any indication of what my life is going to be like when I'm a real spy, it stinks on ice. So let's do this double agent thing. Where do I sign up?"

Murray broke into a big smile. "You have made a very good choice, my friend. C'mon. Let's grab ourselves a sundae and watch the fireworks." He turned his back on me and started toward the door.

I swung the mop handle at the back of his head.

The whole time we'd been in the furnace room, I'd been hoping that, at some point, Erica would suddenly snap to her feet behind Murray's back—revealing that she'd only been *pretending* to be unconscious—and take him out. But she hadn't. Which left me to take care of things and I wasn't going to get a better opportunity than this.

Unfortunately, Murray was onto me; he'd only been faking *his* excitement to see if I was faking mine. Now he dodged as I swung. The mop handle missed his skull by a fraction of an inch.

I staggered off-balance, like a baseball player who had whiffed at a fastball, and when I regained my footing, Murray was aiming both a gun and a look of betrayal at me.

"I can't believe you," he said. "You *lied* to me!"

"All you've done is lie to me!" I shot back.

"That was business," Murray spat. "It wasn't personal. I just gave you the opportunity of a lifetime—and this is how you thank me? You are such a Fleming."

"Better that than a double agent," I shot back.

"At least I'm going to be a *live* double agent," Murray sneered. "And after today everyone will think you're a dead one. You just made the worst decision of what is about to be your very short life."

Keeping his gun trained on me, he pressed a button on the alarm clock, starting the timer at five minutes. Then he stormed out the door and slammed it shut behind him, locking me and Erica inside the room with a ticking bomb.

BOMB DEFUSION

Nathan Hale Administration Building

Subbasement Level 2

February 10

1315 hours

The first time you find yourself locked in a room with a ticking bomb, a lot of thoughts go through your mind.

And a lot of fluid threatens to go through your bladder.

Which means one of the primary thoughts you have is: *Please don't let me wet myself.*

Dying is bad enough, but leaving a corpse with a big damp spot on the pants is just plain embarrassing.

I tried to ignore the urge to pee and deal with the crisis at hand. My first—and only—plan was to rouse Erica; she'd probably been defusing bombs since she was three. I ran to her side and shook her gently, and when that didn't work, I shook her a lot harder. Then I shouted things like, "Erica! If you don't wake up now, we are going to die!" Despite this, she stubbornly remained unconscious.

So I left her in the corner and ran over to examine the bomb. In the movies bombs always seem to be attached to only two wires, a green one and a red one. If you yank the correct one, the bomb doesn't detonate, whereas if you yank the wrong one, it does. Still, that was fifty-fifty—considerably better than my chances of survival if I did nothing.

Unfortunately, a real-life bomb turned out to be far more complicated. There were hundreds of wires snaking about the C4 explosive, in hues ranging from sea green to magenta to cerulean blue. Knowing Murray, I guessed most of them probably didn't do *anything*; he'd only included them to make defusing the bomb maddeningly complex. I had no idea where to even begin.

So I decided to try running away instead. True, this would allow the bomb to detonate and destroy the building, but if I carried Erica, at least we'd be alive. However, Murray had jammed the door shut from the outside. I wedged the mop handle into the gap between the door and the wall and tried to force it open. Instead, the handle shattered into toothpicks.

The clock now said there were ninety seconds left. I'd

squandered three and a half minutes and hadn't made a bit of progress.

Panic set in. I had no idea how to defuse a bomb and no ability to contact anyone who did. And I was quickly running out of time.

I struggled to calm myself. Losing control of myself—or my bladder—wasn't going to help anything. I thought back over my weeks at spy school to see if I could recall *anything* that would be useful in this situation, but nothing came to mind.

Until I thought about the very last conversation I'd had.

Somewhere in there, Murray had said something strange. Something that didn't quite make sense. I struggled to remember it.

The clock showed only forty seconds left until detonation.

In a flash the comment came to me. It was virtually the last thing Murray had said before storming out the door. *At least I'm going to be a live double agent. And after today everyone will think you're a dead one.*

What had he meant by that? I wondered. Why would everyone think *I* was a double agent?

The clock now showed only thirty seconds.

The clock!

I ran back to the bomb to inspect it again. I'd been so focused on the wiring before, I hadn't paid any attention to the timer itself. But now I saw what Murray was talking about.

He'd used my own clock to make the timer.

It was another insidious move on his part. Not only did he plan to kill me, but he planned to frame me as well. After the bomb went off, the government would bring in a Crime Scene Investigation squad to pick over every single piece of debris, no matter how small. And somewhere in the midst of that, they'd eventually find the charred and twisted remains of my clock, which would tie the bomb to me. Once again, Murray would divert attention from himself and make someone else look like the bad guy. Then he'd probably go right back to business as usual.

But there was one thing Murray hadn't counted on. My clock was a piece of junk.

It can't be that simple to stop the bomb, I thought. And yet there was only one thing I could come up with.

There were ten seconds left.

I smacked the clock with an open palm.

It froze at 00:07.

I spent the next seven seconds in agony, fearing that the timer didn't have anything to do with the bomb at all and that I'd be blown sky-high anyhow.

I wasn't.

The bomb didn't detonate.

"What's going on?"

I spun around to find Erica sitting up, groggily clutching her head.

"*Now* you're conscious?" I asked. "You couldn't have come to five minutes ago?"

Erica took in her surroundings and realized what had happened. In an instant she was up on her feet and down to business. "You stopped the bomb?" she asked.

"I think so."

"How?"

"I stopped the timer," I said, trying to sound like it was no big deal.

Erica looked it over, then turned to me, impressed. "Nice work. Although the bomb's still live."

"Do you know how to defuse it?" I asked.

"Of course," she said. "I've been doing this since I was three."

"I guessed as much," I told her.

Erica quickly went to work, removing a pair of wire snippers from her utility belt, inspecting the wires that fed into the timer, tracing them to where they connected to the bomb, and selecting the proper ones to clip.

I stood back to give her room. "How'd you end up down here?"

"I was looking over Chip's evidence against Tina while I was talking to you." Erica snipped an aquamarine wire in two. "But it didn't quite add up, like someone had faked it to make Tina look bad. And then I started thinking, what was the point of putting a bomb in the tunnels anyhow? There's nothing down here really worth destroying . . . although if you built a big enough bomb, like this bad boy here, you could take out the entire building above it." She snipped two more wires, eggshell and crimson. "And the moment I thought that, I realized there wasn't a better target than the Omega conference. So I came down here to see what I could find. Unfortunately, Murray got the jump on me. I was a little distracted by that conversation you and your pal were having about me."

I felt my ears turn red. "Why didn't you tell me what you were doing? I could've helped."

"Guess I just got cocky. You know me and my hero complex." Erica sliced through a tangle of fuchsia wires, then heaved a sigh of relief. "There we go. Bomb's not live anymore." To prove her point, she patted the C4.

I cringed reflexively, but Erica was right. Without the charge connected to it, it was as dangerous as Play-Doh.

Erica ripped off a handful and started toward the door.

"What are you doing?" I asked.

"You want to get out of here or not?" She jammed the explosive into the crack around the dead bolt, backed across the room, and lifted her pant leg to reveal a holster strapped to her leg.

I stared at the gun nestled in it. "That would've been good to know about when Murray was here."

"Why? Did he try to kill you?"

"Uh . . . no. He offered me a job."

Erica turned to me, surprised. "That's interesting." Then she pointed behind the furnace. "You might want to take cover."

I did. She crowded in next to me and shot the C4 around the dead bolt.

There was an explosion. When I peeked out from behind the furnace again, the door was hanging open, a hole the size of a cannonball where the lock had been.

"C'mon," Erica said, racing into the hall. "Before Murray escapes."

I followed right on her heels. "You mean, you *want* my help?"

"I'd say you've proven yourself today." Erica snapped a radio out of her pocket—something else it would have been nice to know about earlier—and spoke into it. "Dad, it's me. There's a bomb in the furnace room under the library. . . . Whoa, don't freak out. It's been neutralized. But someone needs to get down there to remove it. Ben and I are on Subbasement Level Two in pursuit of the mole. His name's Murray Hill. . . . No, I didn't suspect him. . . . Because I didn't, that's why. This is not the time to discuss my analysis skills. I'm hanging up now." She flipped off the radio and gave an exasperated sigh. "Parents. Don't get me started."

"Any idea where Murray is?" I asked.

"Not exactly. Though I'm betting he's still on campus. A good mole wouldn't flee before the bomb goes off—that'd look suspicious. But our guy now *knows* something's wrong. The bomb didn't detonate, which means you and I are still alive—and we know who he is. Now he *has* to run. But he's only known that for . . ." Erica checked her watch.

"Three minutes and thirteen seconds, " I said.

"Right. So we only need to check the cameras." We arrived at the security room from which I'd been kidnapped the day before. The door was still off its hinges. A construction crew was currently repairing it. Erica swung through the gaping hole where the door had been and froze in her tracks. "Nuts."

The security system was down. Every monitor was black. One of the agents who controlled it was frantically leafing through the user's manual. The other was on hold with tech support.

"What happened here?" Erica demanded.

"It just went down," the agent with the manual said.

"About three minutes and fifteen seconds ago?" I asked.

The surprise on her face was all the answer we needed.

"Murray," Erica and I said at the same time.

Erica kicked a trash can angrily. "This campus is two hundred ninety square acres, and he has a huge head start. We'll never find him without the cameras."

"Not necessarily," I said. "You have a phone on you?"

APPREHENSION

Academy Training Grounds
February 10
1340 hours

One of the advantages of being gifted with mathematics is that you never forget a phone number. I called Zoe first, because she always knew everything that was happening on campus. She answered on the third ring. "Hello?" It was lunchtime, and I could hear the usual cacophony of the mess hall around her.

"Zoe, it's Ben."

"Smokescreen! Where have you been? You missed an awesome psychological warfare lecture today."

"Have you seen Murray in the last few minutes?"

Erica led me up a flight of stairs and through a secret doorway to emerge from behind a rack of guns in the armory. Greg Hauser, who worked at the weaponry checkout desk, snapped awake and tried to look like he hadn't been napping on the job, even though there was a strand of drool hanging from his lip.

"Why're you looking for Murray?" Zoe asked.

"Because he's a mole!" I told her.

"Washout? No way. He's way too lazy."

"It's a front. He just tried to blow up the Hale Building and now he's on the run. Do you know where he is or not?"

"I haven't seen him, but hold on." I heard Zoe shout at the top of her lungs, "Has anyone seen Murray?" Someone shouted a response, and then Zoe got back on the phone. "Blackbelt says she saw Murray leaving Bushnell Hall two minutes ago, heading toward the training grounds."

That made sense. The grounds were the opposite direction from the main gate, which had the highest security. Murray was probably looking to sneak through the woods and go over the wall.

"Training grounds," I told Erica.

Erica had already grabbed two M16 rifles off the rack. She tossed one to me along with two extra clips of ammunition. "Let's go."

"Wait!" Hauser protested. "You can't take those without

filling out an H-33 Semiautomatic Request Form!"

"We're on a mole hunt," I said. "C'mon."

"Really?" Hauser looked like a kid who'd just been offered a puppy. "Awesome!"

Erica frowned at me, but she didn't take the time to argue. She simply ran out the door. I followed. Behind us, I could hear Hauser scrambling to grab a weapon of his own.

I got back on the phone. "Zoe, round up everyone you can and get out to the training grounds. We need to find Murray before he gets away."

"Already mobilizing," she said. "Shoot to kill?"

"Uh . . . I don't think that's necessary," I replied. "Maybe just shoot to hobble."

Erica darted across the quadrangle. It took everything I had to keep up with her. She wasn't even breathing hard. "Anyone else you want to invite to the party?" she chided. "Your grandmother, maybe?"

"We can't cover all two hundred ninety acres by ourselves," I panted. "The more eyes we have out here, the better."

Erica tried to give me a disapproving stare, but I could see she knew I was right.

Across the quad from us, the doors to the mess burst open. Students poured out, racing toward the training grounds. The troops had mobilized in a hurry. But then, since this was the first actual call to action at a campus full of wannabe spies, that wasn't really surprising.

Erica and I were well ahead of the others, though. We plunged into the woods.

It had been bitterly cold in the two days since our war game, and what snow remained on the ground was now as hard as cement. Which meant Murray wouldn't have left fresh tracks in it.

"Okay, math whiz," Erica said. "Murray's probably heading from Bushnell toward the closest point on the perimeter, and he has a two-minute jump on us. So what vector gives us the best chance of intercepting him?"

I considered all the variables, then pointed slightly north of due west. Erica adjusted her course and went that way. I followed dutifully.

We moved quickly through the forest, leaping downed trees, ducking branches, skidding on the ice. Erica stayed silent now, conserving her breath and her energy, so I did the same. Many of our fellow students weren't as professional. I could hear them whooping and hollering as they came through the trees, like this was a party rather than a life-or-death mission.

We came upon the gully where Zoe had saved me two days before, which meant we were closing in on the perimeter. I didn't see any evidence of Murray ahead. Not a footprint, not a flash of movement, not a white puff of exhaled breath in the cold. Either he'd made it to wall faster than I'd expected or—

A line of bullets tore across the ground by my feet.

"Ambush!" I dove for cover behind a log.

Erica flattened up against a tree ahead of me.

"Do you see where he is?" I asked her.

"That wasn't from Murray!" she grumbled. "That was friendly fire!" Then she yelled back into the woods. "Lay off the artillery, you dimwits! It's Erica and Ben! We're the good guys!"

"Sorry!" I heard Warren yell. "My bad!"

Erica took off once again.

As I staggered back to my feet, however, the frozen crust of snow beneath me gave way and collapsed into the gully, taking me with it. I tumbled head over heels, smashed through an ice-covered gorse bush, and thudded into the streambed at the bottom.

On the ridgeline above, Erica continued on without so much as a second glance my way. I knew that stopping to help me would have jeopardized any chance she had of catching Murray, but I was still annoyed just the same.

I tried to sit up, but my M16, which was slung over my shoulder, had lodged in some rocks. While I futilely tried to wrench free, the rest of the student body thundered past on the ridge, leaving me behind.

"You all right?"

I turned to find Chip skidding down through the snow toward me.

"Yeah, just stuck," I said. "How'd you . . . ?"

"Hauser called me. I was out on the artillery range. Is Tina on the run?" Chip reached behind me, twisted the gun free, and helped me to my feet.

As I stood, three pounds of snow that had lodged in my jacket slid straight down my back and into my pants, freezing my rear end. "It's not Tina. It's Murray. He set her up."

Chip's jaw practically dropped to his knees. "Murray Hill?! No way. That guy's a total slacker."

"No, he's a master at getting people to underestimate him . . ." I trailed off as my own words sank in. Murray had consistently defied our expectations. He'd convinced everyone he was a washout, fed misinformation to our investigation, and played everyone off each other. Every time we thought we knew what he was going to do, he'd done something else.

A revelation hit me. "He's not going for the wall! He's doubled back!"

I scrambled back up the slope of the gully as fast as I could.

"Wait!" Chip yelled. "How do you know?"

"I just do!" There was no time to explain it to him. I was

only putting it together as I ran. Murray knew he'd been seen heading for the training grounds. Heck, knowing Murray, maybe he'd even *allowed* himself to be seen. Murray wasn't very athletic, though. He knew he didn't have much of a chance of beating Erica to the wall, but if he let her *think* he was heading to the wall—as well as every other student on campus—then he'd leave the path to the front gate wide open. Another diversion. All he'd have to do was find a place to hide, wait for everyone to stampede past him, and then go the other direction.

I raced back through the woods. Behind me, I heard Chip rallying the others in his own personal way. "Turn around, you morons! Ben says Murray's doubled back!"

Far ahead of me, through the trees, I caught a glimpse of Murray climbing down out of a huge oak. He saw me as well, paused while he considered all his options . . . and then fled like a coward.

By the time I emerged from the woods, he was all the way across the quad, skirting the Hale Building on his way toward the front gate.

"Murray! Stop!" Before I even knew what I was doing, I'd swung the gun off my shoulder. "Don't make me use this!"

Murray froze and turned around, allowing me to see he also had a gun in his hand. He aimed right back at me. When he spoke, any friendship he'd ever showed me was gone from his voice. Instead, it was cold and disdainful. "Just back off and let me go, Ben. You don't want to duel me. I know you can't hit the side of a barn from that distance."

Adrenaline coursed through me. My heart hammered in my chest. "Drop your gun, Murray! You're under—"

Murray didn't even let me finish. He opened fire. The first bullets plugged a tree two feet to my right.

I had the chance to shoot back only twice before taking cover. As I dove, I felt a round tear through the sleeve of my jacket and nick my left arm.

Neither of my shots came anywhere close to Murray.

But then, I wasn't aiming for him. He was wrong about one thing. I *could* hit the side of a barn from that distance. More to the point, I could hit the roof of the Hale Building.

The ice on the steep peaked roof had frozen into a crust several inches thick. Both my bullets pounded into it, sparking a network of fractures. A few small glaciers calved free and rocketed off the roof, knocking a dozen massive icicles loose from the eaves en route.

Murray was too busy shooting at me to see it coming. The ice plummeted four stories and flattened him. He faceplanted in the snow, out cold.

I got back to my feet, clutching my arm. In the movies when heroes get winged by bullets, they always shake it off and keep going, like they've been bit by a mosquito. In real life it freaking hurt. It felt like someone had dragged a red-hot poker across my arm—and then punched me a few times for good measure. Thankfully, the wound wasn't too deep and wasn't bleeding too badly.

My heart was pounding so loudly, I didn't hear the other students until they were almost upon me. Chip was the first to arrive, though everyone else wasn't far behind.

"You took out the bad guy?" Chip asked. "Nice!" He raised his hand for a high five.

"Sorry. I can't do that right now," I said, pointing to my wounded arm.

"You got shot?" Zoe was suddenly at my side, her eyes even wider than usual. "Awesome! You're the first in our class to have a battle scar!"

"That wasn't from me, right?" Warren asked. "I mean, back in the woods there, you looked like Murray." He stopped and gaped at Murray across the quad. "Holy cow! You killed him!"

A series of gasps rippled through the crowd.

"Oh, for Pete's sake, relax," Erica sighed, emerging from the trees. "Ripley's not a killer. Murray's unconscious." She stopped beside me and casually inspected my wound. "Aw, that's barely even a scratch. You'll be fine. Just keep pressure on it."

She stared across the snow at the prone body of the mole,

taking everything in. For a few moments she seemed to be her usual, distant self, and I wondered if I'd annoyed her by taking out a bad guy before the entire class when she'd really wanted to do it. But then she turned back to me, patted my shoulder, and smiled. "Good work."

Another series of gasps rippled through the crowd. But now everyone was reacting to Erica. It was the first time many of them had ever seen her touch another human being without being involved in hand-to-hand combat. I think, for a lot of my fellow students, getting Erica to smile was even more impressive than rooting out the mole.

I grinned back. In that instant all my misgivings about the Academy of Espionage flitted away. Sure, the place was poorly managed, run-down, and occasionally life-threatening, but I now felt like I belonged there. I'd proven myself, I'd made friends, I'd earned the respect of the most beautiful girl I'd ever met . . . and I'd thwarted the plot of a criminal mastermind to behead the entire intelligence community of the United States of America.

Regular school couldn't hold a candle to that.

For the first time since I'd arrived on campus, I had a sense that everything was going to work out for me there.

Across the quad Alexander Hale emerged from behind the chemistry building with his gun raised. He cautiously approached Murray's prone body and nudged it with his foot a few times to make sure he was really unconscious.

A door banged open, and a dozen men in three-piece suits and military uniforms poured out of the Hale Building. I recognized the principal's red face among them. "Is that the kid who planted the bomb?" he asked.

"Yes, but he won't be causing us any more trouble." Alexander set one foot upon Murray's haunch and posed dramatically, as if Murray were a grizzly bear he'd downed. "I've neutralized him."

The espionage elite and military leaders reacted with awe. There were shouts of "Well done" and "Bravo!" A few actually applauded.

Alexander bowed dramatically, soaking up their praise.

I turned to Erica, stunned. "Did your father just steal all the credit for what I've done?"

"Looks that way." Erica put a friendly arm around my shoulders and smiled. "Welcome to the wonderful world of espionage."

From:
Office of Intelligence Coordination
The White House
Washington, DC

To:
██████████████████
Director of Internal Investigations
CIA Headquarters
Langley, Virginia

Classified Documents Enclosed
Security Level AA2
For Your Eyes Only

After reading the enclosed transcript, it is evident that considerable work lies ahead of us. It appears that reevaluation of ████████████████████ ███████████, the governance of the Academy of Espionage and the CIA itself is in order. It is shocking and dismaying that the only person in the entire intelligence community to uncover direct evidence of SPYDER is a first year at the academy. Worse, a first year who didn't even officially qualify for entry. Immediate further investigation into this nefarious organization must proceed at all costs.

To that end, I recommend Benjamin Ripley's acceptance into the school be made official. He has certainly earned it. As he remains a target for SPYDER, he should be given K-24 security status—although at this time, it is probably too early to brief him on Operation Enduring Assault. If he knew that ████████████████████████████████████, he'd probably flip out. Instead, allow him to once again believe he is a normal student at the academy whose life is not in the slightest bit of danger.

In addition, as far as the investigation of SPYDER is concerned, I recommend immediate activation of ████████████████, aka Klondike. I am fully aware of the inherent dangers in doing so, but desperate times call for desperate measures. If SPYDER is not neutralized soon, this could portend the end of the intelligence community—and perhaps even the United States of America—as we know it.

My best to Betty and the kids.

██████████████████
Director of Covert Affairs

Haven't spied enough?
Get a supersecret sneak peek
at Ben's next mission in
spy camp!

CONTACT

CIA Academy of Espionage

Washington, DC

Armistead Dormitory

June 10

1500 hours

On the very last day of spy school, my plans for a normal, uneventful summer were completely derailed by the delivery of two letters.

The first was waiting in my room when I returned from my final exam in self-preservation. I had already packed all my belongings, hoping to make a quick exit from campus. The note was perched atop the pile of suitcases.

Up to that point, I'd been having a good day.

To start with, I felt positive about all my exams. I'd been working hard at the academy and had improved in all my classes in the months since I'd arrived. I had jammed on my History of Espionage final, aced Codes and Cryptography, and squeaked through Basic Firearms and Weaponry. (I hadn't scored any bull's-eyes, but unlike some of my fellow first years, I'd at least hit the targets and not accidentally wounded myself.) I'd been most concerned about Intro to Self-Preservation, which had always been my weakest class, though that afternoon I had managed to last for over an hour on the training grounds against a dozen "enemy agents" armed with paintball guns, while much of my class had been smeared with royal blue before five minutes were up. I figured that had to be good for at least an A-minus.

Now, I was relieved to be done with class for the summer. Although I'd miss my friends from the Academy of Espionage, I was eager to head home, see my parents, and have a decent home-cooked meal for the first time in five months. Plus, my thirteenth birthday was only a week away.

I'd made plans to spend it with some old friends, without anyone trying to kill or maim me.

The note, however, suggested there was trouble ahead.

I picked it up gingerly, as though it were explosive. Frankly, I would have preferred finding a bomb in my room. I knew how to handle a bomb. The principal, on the other hand, was far more unpredictable.

I dropped the note in my paper shredder, then burned the remains. It seemed like overkill, but this was standard procedure for all written correspondence at the Academy of Espionage, even Post-it notes. Then I set off for the principal's office.

Outside, the sun was shining brightly, heralding a glorious summer. The academy, which had looked so bleak and dreary in the winter, was now far more attractive. The gothic buildings stood majestically around gorgeous green lawns fringed with flowers. Now that classes had ended, my fellow spies-in-training were reveling in the warm weather. I spotted several friends playing Ultimate Frisbee on the main commons and could hear the distinct rattle of semiautomatic weapons on the firing range in the distance.

"Hey, Smokescreen!" a shrill voice called out. It was Zoe Zibbell, a fellow first year and my best friend, who was with a large group of students. Zoe had christened me "Smokescreen" as she was under the delusion that I was an incredibly talented spy—albeit a spy who often feigned incompetence to make everyone else underestimate him. Any time I displayed my actual incompetence, Zoe inevitably thought it was a ruse. "We're getting up a soccer game on Hammond Quadrangle! Want to play?"

"I can't," I said, then pointed to the Nathan Hale Administration Building. "The principal wants to see me."

Zoe grimaced. So did all the other students. It looked as though I'd told them I had to go face a firing squad. "Is something wrong?"

"I hope not," I said.

"Well, if you feel like it, come find us afterward!" Zoe said, trying her best to be upbeat. "We could use another striker."

I nodded agreement, then entered Administration. Inside, the building was much darker and gloomier—and my mood became much darker and gloomier as well. I trudged up the stairs to the fifth floor, had my retinas scanned, entered the secure area, and presented myself to the two guards flanking the principal's office door.

One frisked me for weapons. "State your name, rank, and business."

"Benjamin Ripley, first-year student. The principal asked to see me."

The second guard picked up a secure phone and

announced my presence. A few seconds later, the door clicked open.

When I entered, the principal was seated behind his desk, making a show of perusing some top secret documents. He might have looked dignified if his toupee hadn't been slightly askew. Or if I hadn't been aware that the principal was incompetent. It might seem surprising that the principal of the CIA's academy for future intelligence agents wasn't intelligent himself—but then, both the CIA and the academy are run by the government. "Sit down, Ripley," the principal told me.

I sat on the ancient couch across from his desk. It smelled like body odor and chloroform.

"My sources tell me you're planning to go home for the summer," the principal said.

"Sources?" I asked. "What sources?"

"Oh, the usual. I'm sure you're aware that we keep close tabs on our student body here. Listening devices, phone taps, that sort of thing."

I hadn't been aware of this at all. "You're tapping my phone?" I asked.

"It's standard procedure. We must keep our guard up at all times. As you know, we've had some trouble with double agents here at the academy."

"Uh, yes. *I* was the one who caught the double agent,"

I said. "You don't really think I'd work for the enemy after that?"

"They did offer you a job."

"Which I turned down. Right before helping defuse a bomb that would have wiped out the heads of every spy organization in the country."

The principal shrugged, unimpressed. "One can never be too cautious," he said. He then leafed through a thick report on his desk. It appeared to contain several transcripts of my private phone calls. "According to this, you intend to spend the summer at the home of your parents and hang out at some place called FunLand with a Mike Brezinski?"

"That's correct," I replied. "Y'know, you could have just *asked* me what I was doing . . ."

"How did you plan on getting away with this?"

"Uh . . . Getting away with what?"

"Avoiding summer school."

I suddenly felt queasy, which happened all too often at spy school. "The academy has summer school?"

"Of course. Evil doesn't take holidays. Why should we?"

"No one ever told me there was summer school," I said.

"Don't be ridiculous. Every new recruit is informed about mandatory summer education during the very first assembly of the school year."

"I wasn't at the first assembly of the school year," I

reminded the principal. "You didn't recruit me until last January."

The principal stared at me blankly for a moment. It was his standard look when he realized that someone had screwed up royally—and it was probably him. I'd seen this expression quite a lot in my five months at spy school. The principal ultimately recovered with his standard response to his screwups: blaming the person who'd been screwed. "Well, you should have figured it out anyhow," he told me. "You're studying to be a spy, for Pete's sake. It's not like the school's existence is a secret."

"The school's existence *is* a secret," I countered.

"I've had enough of your lip!" the principal snapped. "Would you like to begin summer school on probation?"

I shook my head, then realized something. "All the other students have been packing their things. Aren't they attending summer school too?"

"Absolutely. Everyone at the academy is required to attend summer courses. They're just not taught *here*."

"Then where are they taught?"

"At our wilderness education facility."

"Wilderness education?" I repeated.

"Yes," the principal said. "During the summer months, we shift from classroom subjects to focus more on physical training and outdoor survival schools. After all, ninety-nine percent of the world is outdoors. A good spy needs to know how to get along there."

"So . . . it's kind of like spy camp."

"It's not camp!" the principal shouted. "It's an elite wilderness survival training facility. It merely happens to *look* like a camp. And as far as your family, friends, or anyone else knows, you will be attending a camp. The Happy Trails Sleepaway Camp for Boys and Girls." The principal rooted around in his desk drawer until he found a document, which he then slid across the desk to me.

It was a single page with the address of the point in Washington, DC, where I would meet the official academy vehicle for transportation to the camp, and a list of survival supplies to bring. At the bottom, as with all documentation at spy school, there was a directive to memorize the contents and then destroy it.

"When does it start?" I asked.

"In three days," the principal replied. "Go home and have a nice weekend with your family. But don't tell anyone about the true nature of this camp . . ."

"Or you'll have to kill me," I finished. I knew the routine.

"Exactly. We'll see you on Monday at oh nine hundred hours sharp." The principal returned to his top secret documents, as though I had suddenly ceased to exist. Our meeting was over.

I let myself out of his office and headed back to my room.

My immediate reaction to the news that I had mandatory summer school was annoyance and frustration. I'd been working hard for the past five months and I missed my family and friends; I felt I deserved a few weeks off from my studies. But as I crossed campus, my mood began to change. While my first few weeks at spy school had been difficult—I'd nearly been assassinated, kidnapped, and blown up—things had got much better after people had stopped trying to kill me. I had come to enjoy school and had made a lot of friends. In fact, for the first time in my life, I was regarded as somewhat cool; preventing the destruction of your school and capturing the agent responsible is a great boon to your social life. Meanwhile, back home, my spy student identity was still a secret. Everyone thought I was attending some lame science school. I'd probably be even less popular than I had been before I'd left. Thus, the idea of spending more time with my fellow spies-to-be wasn't so bad. And the fact that I'd be doing it outdoors, rather than cooped up inside dingy old classrooms, made it sound even better.

By the time I got back to my dorm room, I was thinking a summer at spy camp might be kind of fun.

And then I found the second letter.

It was exactly where the first one had been, perched atop

all my suitcases. Even though I'd locked the door to my room before going to see the principal.

Hey Ben!

Just wanted you to know we'll be coming for you soon.

Your pals at SPYDER

I sat on my bed, feeling as though the wind had been knocked out of me.

SPYDER was the evil organization that had planted a mole in the school, sent an assassin to my room, and tried to take out every leader in the intelligence community with a bomb. I hadn't heard a thing from them since helping to defeat their nefarious plans.

Maybe this summer wasn't going to be so much fun after all.

Mystery, murder, mayhem.
That's no excuse to be rude.

★ "A sharp-witted debut . . . one that will leave readers eagerly awaiting subsequent installments."

—*Publishers Weekly*, starred review, on *Murder Is Bad Manners*

When a wealthy recluse opens her home to a chosen few, secrets hide around every corner.

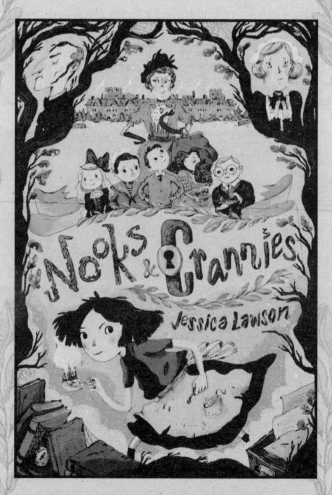